UPSETS,
COMEBACKS
& TURNAROUNDS

David N. Hunter, Sr.

PAGE PUBLISHING, INC.
New York, NY

First originally published by Page Publishing, Inc. 2018

ISBN 978-1-64082-090-6 (Paperback)
ISBN 978-1-64082-091-3 (Digital)

Printed in the United States of America

CONTENTS

DEDICATION

First and foremost, this book is dedicated to all who have overcome overwhelming obstacles and to those who have overwhelming obstacles yet to overcome. This is to all who were not favored to win, to those who were voted least likely to succeed, and to the long list of the unlikeliest, the unmentionables, and the underrateds. In other words, the underdogs!

This book is also a tribute to all of the biblical long-shots. To all who "didn't stand a chance;" and yet, someway, somehow, they found a way to believe God for, or experience, a miracle. This is a telling of their side of the story, how God executed righteousness and judgment for them for "He executes righteousness and judgment for all who are oppressed" (Psalm 103:6).

An underdog is "a person who is expected to lose in a contest or conflict or is a victim of social or political injustice."[1] Because of sin, we all are spiritual underdogs. Jesus came and won the day for us because we could not fight, much less win, on our own.

Likewise, those who have overcome seemingly insurmountable odds to experience overwhelming victories give us an example to go by. Their battles are our battles; their victories, our victories. At one point in their lives, Esther and Elijah, Jonathan and Jehoshaphat, Leah and others alike, all were spiritually bereft of hope and brimming with despair. While defunct of faith, God stepped in and reversed their circumstances for good. Reading their stories is rich spiritual food and fodder for all of us who need encouragement and a spiritual shot in the arm. Just as the hymn writer wrote, we take

---

[1]   http://dictionary.reference.com/browse/underdog

solace in the reflection of their triumphs, knowing that what God has done, He is yet able to do again.

> *It is no secret what God can do.*
> *What He's done for others He will do for you.*[2]

---

[2]   Stuart Hamblen, *"It is no Secret (What God Can Do)"*, 1952.

FOREWORD

Every sports fan loves a great comeback. When a favorite athlete or team comes from behind and turns certain defeat into an improbable victory, it is the stuff of which legends and reputations are made. Fortunately for us all, fantastic finishes are not limited to the court, the field or the ice. In truth, some of the most remarkable comebacks ever recorded involve ordinary people whose lives are touched in unexpected ways by the hand of an extraordinary God.

Upsets, Comebacks & Turnarounds examines the lives of five everyday men and women of the Bible who overcame the odds and emerged as winners. Each had personal challenges, obstacles and limitations. None was a champion from birth. All were recipients of heavenly intervention from a God who is no respecter of persons, but who greatly esteems humility and faith. Their stories provide hope that no matter the score or the time remaining on the clock, there is an all-powerful God who remains mindful of us. A God for whom the miraculous is the routine. A God who stands ready to reveal Himself in life-altering ways, going all-in for those who others have counted out.

Jeff Fannell, Esq.
Jeff Fannell & Associates, LLC

ACKNOWLEDGMENTS

I want to extend my deepest gratitude to my family and friends who assisted me and encouraged me with this work.

To my wife, Lisa, thank you for being my primary prayer partner, companion, sounding board, and best friend. To my two sons, David Jr. and Daniel, thank you for your input, insight, and support along the way. To my "editor," Rev. Jane Collinson, thank you. Many times you read this manuscript for consistency, correctness, and continuity. Your love, care, and commitment to see this work through is appreciated. I owe you much love.

And finally, to my parents, the late Chaplain Elmer Nathaniel Hunter and Mother Lerotha Audrey Hunter, thank you. You nurtured me, instilled in me a love for God and for people. Your demonstration of giving your best, doing your best, and being the best provided me with all of the necessary ingredients to create this book—*Upsets, Comebacks, and Turnarounds.*

Your legacy of love lives on through me. I miss you so much.

CHAPTER 1

Unlikely Leah Comes From Behind

When the Lord saw that Leah was unloved, He opened her womb;

And she conceived again, gave birth to a son, and said, "This time I will praise the Lord." Therefore she named him Judah. Then Leah stopped having children.

—Genesis 29:31–35

Unlikely Champions

Not too long ago, "just one month after returning to competition, the unseeded Kim Clijsters, 26, who hadn't played enough tennis to warrant a ranking, defeated ninth-seeded Caroline Wozniacki of Denmark, 7-5, 6-3" and won the U.S. Open. It was "the mother of all comebacks." Tennis officials "granted her a wild-card entry since her lack of a ranking meant she wouldn't otherwise qualify."[3] After giving birth to her first child, Kim had hoped to "simply regain the rhythm of the game with an eye of returning to top form in 2010."

---

[3] Liz Clarke, "For Clijsters, It's the Mother of All Comebacks," *The Washington Post*, September 14, 2009.

Instead, she surprised even herself and went farther and advanced further than she could ever dream in a very short time.

Like this tennis champion who came out of nowhere and stunned the tennis world to do what no one expected her to do, Leah was a wild-card entry in the history of Israel and became the mother of the tribe of Judah. Genesis 29 tells us she became a victorious champion who trusted God to turn her situation around quickly.

Leah vs. Rachel

Leah's story is an unprecedented upset victory, a come-from-behind triumph of epic proportions, a tremendous turnaround. While Genesis 29 features Jacob as the lead protagonist, with Laban and Rachel as supporting actors, our focus here is on Leah. The Bible account is full of contrasts between Leah and her younger sister, Rachel, and between her father, Laban, and Jacob, the husband she shares with Rachel.

The complex background of the story is this: Jacob comes to town running for his life but not necessarily looking for a wife. He has just deceived his father and tricked his older brother Esau out of the birthright and the blessing; he leaves his parents' house at their direction in search of relatives and finds them in Haran. He first meets Rachel at a well and falls head over heels for her. He then meets Laban, and in Laban, the crafty Jacob has met his match. Finally we are introduced to Leah, but scripture does not record the meeting of Leah and Jacob, the subjects of our study.

Scripture gives us a stark contrast and a sheer contradiction of Leah and Rachel as the description of the two sisters is telling. Leah's name could mean "weary," "dull," or even "wild cow." Rachel means ewe lamb.[4] In the King James Version, verse 17 states that "Leah was tender eyed; but Rachel was beautiful and well favored." The RSV states that "Leah's eyes were weak, but Rachel was beautiful and lovely." The Message Bible tells us that "Rachel was stunningly beautiful." The difference in appearance between the two sisters is

---

[4] International Standard Bible Encyclopaedia, Electronic Database Copyright © 1996, 2003, 2006 by Biblesoft, Inc., *"Leah."*

emphasized and seems to hint of other distinctions as well. "Rachel was beautiful in both face and form, much more so than Leah apparently, and much more desirable."[5] We are left to surmise that they were polar opposites.

Contrary to Morris, Clarke tells us that "I believe the word 'tender-eyed' (KJV) means just the reverse of the signification generally given it. The design of the inspired writer is to *compare* both the sisters so that the balance may appear greatly in favor of Rachel."[6] Leah's "eyes were lacking that luster which always and everywhere is looked upon as a conspicuous part of female beauty. Josephus (Ant, I, xix 7) says of her, *ten opsin ouk euprepe*, which may safely be rendered, 'she was of no comely countenance.'"[7] While Leah may not have been as lovely as Rachel, both were unmarried and childless.

Leah's Fruitfulness

A son was the sign of strength, but at this point in the biblical narrative, no sons of Laban are mentioned (ref. Genesis 30:35–31:1: sons are mentioned when Jacob's eldest son was around twelve). At this point, however, without sons, his aim was to marry off his daughters—Leah first, then Rachel. To remain unmarried was unthinkable in the culture of Israel. "Marriage was not considered a religious rite but a 'civil contract.' It was the normal way of life: in Israel celibacy has no status and not to be married was considered a humiliation."[8] Not only so, but to be husbandless meant you were childless. The Psalmist tells us that "children are a heritage of the Lord: and the fruit of the womb is his reward" (Psalm 127:3, KJV). Certainly Leah, and Rachel for that matter, both desired husbands. Yet, "it is not clear why [Leah] was unable to find a husband; quite possibly it was

---

[5]   Henry M. Morris, *The Genesis Record*. (Grand Rapids: Baker Book House, 1976), p. 460.

[6]   Adam Clarke, *Clarke's Commentary*. (New York, Abingdon Press, Volume I, 1973), p. 182.

[7]   International Standard Bible Encyclopaedia, Electronic Database Copyright © 1996, 2003, 2006 by Biblesoft, Inc, "*Leah*."

[8]   Philip J. King and Lawrence E. Stager, *Life in Biblical Israel* (Louisville: Westminster John Knox Press), 2001, p. 56.

because none of the eligible men of Haran were acceptable to her father."[9] "Both of his daughters were apparently well beyond the age at which woman usually married, and Laban may have become quite concerned about finding a husband for Leah, the older sister."[10] This scenario of "singleness" for these two women is certainly contrary to the custom.

Trick Plays

Jacob agrees to work seven years for Rachel. He "asks for Rachel as a reward for service instead of paying the usual marriage price."[11] After serving the agreed upon seven years, Jacob demands Laban to give him Rachel and he is short and to the point: "Give me my wife" (v. 21). At the marriage feast, Laban presents not Rachel, but a veiled, hidden Leah to his unwitting nephew. Thus, this upheaval upstaged and upset Jacob, and it set the stage for Leah's miracle. Leah was used by her father to make a fool of Jacob by being sent into his tent the night he thought he was marrying his beloved Rachel. "The deceit leads to an intolerable home life."[12]

According to Laban's testimony, Leah, the elder sister, is to be wed first, then Rachel. One source states that "the custom Laban refers to is not otherwise known."[13] There is further evidence that Laban was only claiming adherence to a local custom for his own benefit and for the sake of convenience. "The excuse and atonement Laban made for the cheat [was lame]. First, the excuse was frivolous: 'it must not be so done in our country' (v. 26). We have reason to think there was no such custom of his country as he pretends; only he banters Jacob with it, and laughs at his mistake. [It is noted that] those that can do wickedly and then think to turn it off with a jest,

9   Henry M. Morris, *The Genesis Record* (Grand Rapids: Baker Book House), 1976, p. 460.

10   Ibid.

11   Herbert G. May and Bruce M. Metzger, Eds. *The New Oxford Annotated Bible with the Apocrypha*, (New York: Oxford University Press), p. 36.

12   David Alexander and Pat Alexander, *Eerdmans Handbook to the Bible* (Grand Rapids, William Eerdmans Publishing Company, 1973), p. 145.

13   Ibid.

though they may deceive themselves and others, [they] will find at last that God is not mocked. But if there had been such a custom, and he had resolved to observe it, he should have told Jacob so when he undertook to serve him for his younger daughter."[14]

However, according to Barnes, "It is still the custom not to give the younger in marriage before the older, unless the latter be deformed or in some way defective."[15] Clarke agrees with Barnes and states that "Herodotus mentions a very singular custom among the Babylonians."[16] "We sympathize when, at the end of the seven years of service, the wrong woman is pawned off on him, with the excuse that custom (attested by the practice of other peoples) demands that the elder shall be married before the younger."[17]

Nonetheless, "Scripture does not tell us what the feelings between the two sisters may have been; no doubt Leah was somewhat jealous of Rachel, but there is no reason to think she would have relished hurting her sister in any way. She was, of course, being obedient to her father in going through with the rickety ruse and deceitful deception; but she surely realized it was wrong and cruel. Unless she wanted Jacob so badly herself that all other considerations were forgotten, it may have been a very difficult night for her too."[18]

Warren Wiersbe disagrees. "I feel that Leah was a willing accomplice, happy to get a hard-working husband like Jacob, who would inherit Isaac's wealth and enjoy the covenant blessings of Abraham. Certainly she knew that Rachel would also be part of the bargain but was willing to risk whatever problems might ensue. Leah may have

---

[14] Matthew Henry's Commentary on the Whole Bible, PC Study Bible Formatted Electronic Database Copyright © 2006 by Biblesoft.

[15] Barnes' Notes, Electronic Database Copyright © 1997, 2003, 2005, 2006 by Biblesoft, Inc.

[16] Adam Clarke. *Clarke's Commentary.* (New York, Abingdon Press, Volume I, 1973), p. 182.

[17] Frederick Carl Eislen, Edwin Lewis and David G. Downey, Eds. *The Abingdon Bible Commentary.* (New York: Abington-Cokesbury Press, 1929), p. 238.

[18] Henry M. Morris, *The Genesis Record* (Grand Rapids: Baker Book House, 1976), p. 462.

'borrowed' some of her sister's garments and even learned to imitate some of her personal mannerisms. If so, she was treating Jacob just the way he had treated his father when he pretended to be Esau."[19]

Another view of Leah's plight suggests that "had Leah so desired, she could easily have revealed the plot, but that would have embarrassed Laban before his guests and probably led to Jacob's being banished from the home without his beloved Rachel. Then for the rest of her life, Leah would have had to live with a disappointed sister and an angry father, who would devise some means to get even with his elder daughter. No, revealing the scheme just wasn't worth it."[20] The enemy has a tendency to try and trip us and trap us in his plots and ploys. But God has a way of plowing every plot and tripping every trap set against us.

Willing or not, Leah was in the middle of a mess. Clearly, Leah was a victim of her circumstances. She was a leading candidate for the title of "most unlikely" and in much need of a spiritual reversal; Leah was hated by her husband, disrespected by her father, and tolerated by her sister. Leah played second fiddle to a jealous sister and then learned to endure as the second string wife of a possibly emotionally abusive husband. "While the only specific weakness that is mentioned is that she was 'tender eyed,' this does not necessarily mean that she was 'weak eyed,' however, as some have interpreted it; it could mean that she did not have eyes as dark and lustrous as those of Rachel."[21] The New Living Translation says that "there was no sparkle in Leah's eyes." And there are times when there is no sparkle in our eyes as we are emotionally mistreated and spiritually maltreated, bruised, battered, and beaten by those whom we love and cherish.

On the Sideline Hated and Hurting

Leah had been refused and rejected and thus was subjected to suffer from the fear of rejection. She may have had low self-esteem

[19] The Bible Exposition Commentary: Old Testament © 2001-2004 by Warren W. Wiersbe

[20] Ibid.

[21] Henry M. Morris, *The Genesis Record* (Grand Rapids: Baker Book House, 1976), p. 460.

and certainly wanted to be accepted so badly that she became a people pleaser. She may have also suffered from affirmation depravation. She sought to please her husband, and she longed for his affirming touch and his reassuring words. While the two were intimate, the intimacy was not based on love, but on lust. And sexual intercourse is a cheap substitute for love. Instead of Jacob giving her affection, God gave her sons.

The KJV states that Leah was "hated" (v. 31), i.e., she was loved less than Rachel. "By becoming a party to a heartless fraud, she sowed confusion into her relationships. And Rachel, the beloved wife, was denied the blessing of children, so coveted by the ancient Hebrew mothers (v. 31). Both had trials, though of a different kind."[22] The New Living Translation states that "now the Lord saw that Leah was unloved, and He opened her womb" (v. 31). While the word "hated" may be too strong, the aforementioned contrast given between Leah and Rachel, and Jacob's contrasting affection for each sister, should not be lost on the reader. The genuine meaning of the original Hebrew word is disputed. "The word simply signifies a less degree of love. So it is said in v. 30 Jacob loved Rachel more that Leah."[23] Whether it was hatred or "less loved," it is clear that Leah was treated differently, and she felt it.

In spite of the mistreatment by her husband and family, the Lord had mercy on her soul and extended grace to her spirit. The Lord returned compassion when she did not complain and showed her favor. "Leah's circumstances mirror those of Hannah and support "the belief that the Lord protects the less-favored wife and makes her fruitful."[24] By extension, we can joy in the fact that God protects the less favored and elevates those who are looked down upon but instead look up to Him.

---

[22] Matthew Henry's Commentary on the Whole Bible, PC Study Bible Formatted Electronic Database. Copyright © 2006 by Biblesoft.

[23] Adam Clarke, *Clarke's Commentary* (New York, Abingdon Press, Volume I, 1973), p. 184.

[24] George Arthur Buttrick, *The Interpreters Bible, Volume 1.* (Nashville: Abingdon Press, 1991), p. 703.

God Sees The Entire Playing Field

Leah was emotionally bruised, battered, and beaten. She was a broken reed. She must have felt used, alone, and despised as she was stuck between no-place and nowhere with no-one to turn to. But, thankfully, God saw her plight, intervened on her behalf, and turned her situation around. Thankfully for Leah and for all others, God executes righteousness and judgment for all who are oppressed. And Leah was oppressed. We are comforted in knowing that "every stroke given to the weakest member of Christ's body reaches the living Head, and every wrong inflicted upon the little ones that believe on Him is an injury to Himself."[25] God sees all, and He saw Leah's broken, wounded spirit. Vengeance is mine I will repay, says the Lord. Speaking of Himself, Jesus quotes Elijah:

> *He will not break a bruised reed*
> *Or quench a smoldering wick,*
> *Till he brings justice to victory. (Matthew 12:20,*
> *RSV)*

It is significant to note that "the Lord saw" Leah's affliction. "The eye of the Lord is upon the sufferer. It is remarkable that both the narrator and Leah employ the proper name of God [Lord], which makes the performance of promise a prominent feature of his character. This is appropriate in the mouth of Leah, who is the mother of the promised seed. [What did the Lord see?] He saw 'that Leah was hated' or less loved than Rachel. He therefore recompenses her for the lack of her husband's affections by giving her children while Rachel was barren . . . Leah had qualities of heart, if not of outward appearance, which commanded esteem. She had learned to acknowledge the Lord in all her ways."[26]

---

[25] Herbert Lockyer, *All the Miracles of the Bible* (Grand Rapids: Zondervan Publishing Co.) 1965, p. 272.

[26] Barnes' Notes, Electronic Database. Copyright © 1997, 2003, 2005, 2006 by Biblesoft, Inc.

Leah's Victory: Sons

After the embarrassment of being deceptively given to Jacob, the Lord opened Leah's womb and she gave birth to four sons and, later, two more sons and one daughter (chapter 31). In spite of all that she went through, Leah had one thing in her favor; she had one thing going her way: Leah could bear children. "Leah was blessed with children which compensated her for the loss of her husband's love. The names of the four sons successively born to her were all significant, and [they] betoken that pious habit of mind which recognized the hand of God in all that befell her."[27] "Names are significant; and those which Leah gave to her sons were expressive of her varying feelings of thankfulness or joy, or allusive to circumstance in the history of the family. There was piety and wisdom in attaching a signification to names as it tended to keep the bearer in remembrance of his duty and the claims of God."[28]

Leah "called the first-born Reuben [which in Hebrew means] 'see ye a son.' A second meaning of the name is that he has seen my misery, because the reason given for so calling him is 'the Lord hath looked upon my affliction,' which in Hebrew is *ra'ah be'onyi*, literally, 'He hath seen my affliction.'"[29] "Simeon means 'hearing' for God had heard her earnest prayer and heard her weary cry. The third son was named Levi which means 'joined.' Now, surely, would the breach be healed and the husband and wife joined together by this threefold cord. The fourth she called Judah which means 'praise,' as if recording her thankfulness that she had won the affections of her husband by bearing to him so many sons . . . for Leah was still hoping that Jacob would love her for the sons she had borne him. It must have

---

[27] T. H. Leale, *The Biblical Illustrator,* http://ibiblestudies.com/authors/leale.htm

[28] Robert Jamieson, A.R. Fausset and David Brown, *Commentary Critical Explanation on the Whole Bible. Logos* Bible Software.

[29] International Standard Bible Encyclopaedia, Electronic Database Copyright © 1996, 2003, 2006 by Biblesoft, Inc.

been painful for her to have to give herself to a husband who was only doing his duty and not sharing his affection."[30]

"The third and fourth children mothered by Leah are Levi and Judah (29:34–35). From Levi comes the line of priests. From Judah comes the line of kings and eventually Jesus. Two of the most significant institutions in the Old Testament have their origin in an unwanted marriage."[31]

Leah must have been a devout, praying woman for she declared that the Lord "has heard that I am hated." Not only did God see Leah's affliction, but He heard Leah's cry for help. To Leah's credit, after giving birth to three sons, after trying things her way, she turned to the Lord. Instead of complaining, she rejoiced. Instead of whining and playing the victim, she shouted and became the victor. Instead of hanging her head, she lifted her hands in surrender to God. She chose to praise the Lord.

Leah turned her sorrow into dancing. Instead of accusing God falsely, she testified of His goodness. Leah said, "Now I will praise the Lord (KJV)." "The birth of her fourth son seemed to bring a new joy to her life, for she called him Judah, which comes from the Hebrew word meaning 'praise.' Instead of complaining to the Lord about her unresponsive husband, she was now praising the Lord for His blessings. 'This time I will praise the Lord.'"[32] The LXX (The Greek Old Testament, Septuagint) combines the "now" and this time by quoting Leah this way: "Now yet again this time will I give thanks to the Lord" (Genesis 29:35).

Now is the Arrival Time of God

The word "now" is a literary connective and it symbolizes progression. Leah had progressed from the past through the present and

---

[30] Warren W. Wiersbe, *Be Authentic (Genesis 25–50): Exhibiting Real Faith in the Real World*, (Colorado Springs: David C. Cook, 1997), p. 52.

[31] Victor Hamilton, *Handbook on the Pentateuch* (Grand Rapids: Baker Academic, 1982, 2005), p. 114.

[32] Keil and Delitzsch Commentary on the Old Testament: New Updated Edition, Electronic Database. Copyright © 1996 by Hendrickson Publishers, Inc.

was living not temporally but eternally. Leah decided that "now" was the time to praise. She said not later, when my problem is fixed; not later when Jacob decides to love me; not later, when my relationship with my sister is healed; she said "now" is the time. "Now" does not look backward or forward but heavenward. "Now" is time eternal.

"Now" is the arrival time of God. "Now" is the time to give unto the Lord the glory due His name. "Now" is the time to worship. "Now" is the time to give our hearts to the Lord. Leah decided not to wait until things got better. She decided not to wait until she got herself together. Leah decided not to wait until the rain stopped or until the sun came out. She decided to praise God—now. Now is the time! "Now will I praise the Lord" is Leah's monumental confession that stands as the hallmark and touchstone of her faith.

The writer of Hebrews says, "Now faith is the assurance of things hoped for, the conviction of things not seen" (Hebrews 11:1–2, RSV). Paul exhorts the church at Corinth this way: "Now thanks be unto God, which always causeth us to triumph in Christ" (2 Corinthians 2:14, KJV). And to the church at Ephesus, Paul stresses "now" this way: "Now unto him that is able to do exceeding abundantly above all that we ask or think, according to the power that worketh in us" (Ephesians 3:20, KJV).

Don't Retaliate, Celebrate!

In spite of being mistreated, Leah's life and eternal legacy turned all the way around because of her faith in God. Leah staged one of the greatest comebacks in biblical history by not giving in and not giving up in the face of opposition. "God saw the suffering Leah endured and he blessed her above her more attractive sister. Leah held a special place because of the sons she had. Her son Levi became the father of the priestly tribe of Israel and his descendants include Moses, Aaron, Elizabeth the mother of John the Baptist, Barnabas, and Peter. From the descendants of Judah came King David and Jesus, the Son of God."[33] Further, at the end of their lives, Jacob chose to bury his wife Leah in the family burial plot in the cave of Machpelah.

---

[33]   http://gardenofpraise.com/bibl83s.htm

There they buried Abraham and Sarah his wife;
there they buried Isaac and Rebekah his wife; and
there I buried Leah. (Genesis 49:31, RSV)

In spite of being used and abused, Leah found strength and decided not to retaliate, but to celebrate. Leah chose to put on the "garment of praise for the spirit of heaviness" (Isaiah 61:3). Leah chose to set her affection on things above, not on things on the earth" (Colossians 3:2). "Thus the lesson is brought home to us that Yahweh has a special and kindly regard for the lowly and despised, provided they learn, through their troubles and afflictions, to look to Him for help and success. It seems that homely Leah was a person of deep-rooted piety and therefore better suited to become instrumental in carrying out the plans of Yahweh than her handsome, but worldly-minded sister Rachel."[34]

However, contrary to this opinion, the meek and modest can receive mercy without leaning a single life lesson. And good can come from the worldly minded ones too. How? Because God's mercy is not dependent upon our ability to learn from our mistakes. Sometimes He keeps blessing us just because He loves us.

Leah's story is our story, when we turn from trying to please people. Leah's victory is our victory when we cease from our wandering from Him and struggling to win the affection of others instead of setting our affection on things above. Leah's turnaround is our turnaround when we decide to praise the Lord.

The soul that on Jesus hath leaned for repose
I will not, I will not desert to its foes;
That soul, though all hell should endeavor to shake,
I'll never, no never, no never forsake![35]

---

[34] International Standard Bible Encyclopaedia, Electronic Database Copyright © 1996, 2003, 2006 by Biblesoft, Inc., "*LEAH.*"

[35] John Rippon, "*How Firm a Foundation,*" 1787.

Spiritual Lessons

1. God works all things together for our good. (Romans 8:28)
2. What others mean for evil, God can use for good. He can't make evil good, but God can bring good out of evil. (Genesis 50:20)
3. We will never fully please people, so we should be comforted by God's approval. (Genesis 29:35)
4. We cannot run from our sin or our trials, but we must run to Him. (Jacob and Leah)
5. God has a master plan and we must trust Him to see it through to completion. (Jesus is the Lion of the Tribe of Judah, Revelation 5:5).

CHAPTER 2

Jonathan Jolts the Juggernauts

Jonathan said to his armor bearer, "Come on now, let's go across to these uncircumcised pagans. Maybe God will work for us. There's no rule that says God can only deliver by using a big army. No one can stop God from saving when he sets his mind to it."

—1 Samuel 14:6–7, NLT

Danny Manning and the Miracles

The path to victory was an uphill climb. Danny Manning, the star forward for the University of Kansas, "rose far above Oklahoma to lift upstart Kansas to the NCAA Championship. It was an unprecedented one-man show. The Oklahoma Sooners could only watch in awe. Danny Manning scored 31 points to go with his career-high 18 rebounds, 5 steals, and 2 blocked shots" as the Kansas Jayhawks shocked the college basketball world and defeated the heavily favored Oklahoma Sooners to win the 1988 Men's Basketball Title.[36] This miraculous upset victory by Danny Manning and his supporting

---

[36] Curry Kirkpatrick, "A One Man Show" *Sports Illustrated,* April 11, 1988, p. 18.

cast, "the Miracles," is a Cinderella story of how one man, against all odds, can make a difference.

Likewise, Jonathan literally climbed his way to biblical prominence as he rose above his father, his fellows, and his own fears; he ascended the jagged cliffs of Gibeah and attacked an unsuspecting garrison of the Philistine army to affect a stunning upset victory. Like Danny Manning's story, Jonathan's was a "Cinderella story" of how one man, against all odds, can make a difference. Jonathan acted when neither his father the king nor any other soldier would. Because of his boldness, courage, and faith in God, the victory was won.

Jonathan's Heroics

Jonathan's heroics in 1 Samuel 14 pave the way for an unthinkable upset victory, a convincing comeback, a titanium turnaround. King Saul dominates the bulk of 1 Samuel, which centers on his reign as Israel's first king and the transition between Saul and David. In between and in the middle of this pair of polar opposite patriarchs, we have Jonathan, the son of Saul and the friend of David, as he is strung between the two personalities and leadership extremes. "Jonathan is best remembered as the friend of David. He exemplified all that is noblest in friendship— warmth of affection, unselfishness, helpfulness, and loyalty."[37] In this sense, Jonathan is a figure of Christ, "the friend that sticks closer than a brother" (Proverbs 18:24). Jonathan loved David how scripture implores us to love each other for "a friend loves at all times, and a brother is born for adversity" (Proverbs 17:17, RSV).

Here, we focus on God and one man. This is the story of how God used Jonathan in a most unusual way. At the beginning of 1 Samuel 14, we read of a stand-off between the Israelites and the Philistines who were Israel's arch-rival and perennial foe. This stalemate was a lopsided one because it adversely affected the Israelite army. After only two years in office, Saul proved that he was not a spiritual but a carnal leader. He had penchant for doing nothing

---

[37] Merrill C. Tenney, *Pictorial Bible Dictionary* (Nashville, TN: The Southwestern Company, 1976), p. 444.

or the wrong thing. For his standing army, Saul chose three thousand men and put a thousand of them under Jonathan's charge. Yet Saul's troops had dwindled from three thousand down to six hundred. Over two-thirds of the force was hiding in dens and caves of the earth; much worse, some had even defected to the other side. Hence, given the bleak state of affairs, Jonathan knew that he had to do something. Doing nothing was not an option. Something had to be done, now! Jonathan's wisdom and determination led to a victory for Israel beyond comparison.

Victories are individual and corporate. Most of Israel's victories over their enemies came after corporate battles. The Philistines constantly provoked them, and time and again they were a thorn in their side. This time, in order to deliver His people from their adversaries, we see how God chose to go another way—first with Jonathan in 1 Samuel 14, and then with David in 1 Samuel 17. God anointed each to win the battle because of their faith, their courage, and the power of God within them. Jonathan heard the same voice that came to Zerubbabel: "It is not by force nor by strength, but by my Spirit, says the Lord of Heaven's Armies" (Zechariah 4:6–7, New Living Translation).

Jonathan's spiritual heroism is exemplary. Against the contrast of his spiritually dark, disobedient, and deceitful father, Jonathan beams as bright and shining star. Jonathan was not content with allowing the enemy to have the upper hand. "The focus in this chapter (14) is on Jonathan, Saul's oldest son, who had won the first major battle against the Philistines; but his father had taken the credit (13:1–7). It's a remarkable blessing of the grace of God that a man like Saul should have a son as magnificent as Jonathan."[38]

Warfare is armed conflict. Just as natural battles require armor, spiritual battles require armor as well. The weapons of our warfare are not carnal, and we are to put on the whole armor of God (Ephesians 6:10). Scripture tells us that only Saul and Jonathan had swords (1 Samuel 13:22); the rest of the army must have used makeshift weapons. The victory is all the more dramatic because "in this

---

[38] The Bible Exposition Commentary: Old Testament © 2001–2004 by Warren W. Wiersbe.

rout, the only weapons the Israelites had were farming implements (I Samuel 13:20), Saul and Jonathan alone being armed with swords and spears."[39] Jonathan attacked and defeated the Philistine Garrison at Gibeah. In response, the Philistines set out to attack the Israelites.

> *And the Philistines mustered to fight with Israel, thirty thousand chariots, and six thousand horsemen, and troops like the sand on the seashore in multitude; they came up and encamped in Michmash, to the east of Beth-a'ven.*
>
> *When the men of Israel saw that they were in straits (for the people were hard pressed), the people hid themselves in caves and in holes and in rocks and in tombs and in cisterns, or crossed the fords of the Jordan to the land of Gad and Gilead. Saul was still at Gilgal, and all the people followed him trembling. (1 Samuel 13:5–7)*

Fear vs. Faith

Fear and doubt are the enemies of faith and drive. They combine to hamper our progression and God's provision. They put a choke hold on and hinder the move of God. Because the Philistines marshaled so many men and machinery, for fear "the people followed (Saul) trembling" (13:7) and then, when Saul did not know what to do, "the people were scattered from him" (13:8). Fear causes us to tremble when we should stand firm; doubt scatters our fortitude when we should be gathering strength.

We now come to what the New Living Translation calls "Jonathan's Daring Plan." The King James Version states that "now it came to pass upon a day" (v. 1). It came to Jonathan that the status quo was unacceptable. He saw the army dwindling and dismay kindling. Jonathan's keen gift of discernment is later apparent in his

---

[39] Merrill C. Tenney, *Pictorial Bible Dictionary* (Nashville, TN: The Southwestern Company, 1976), p. 444.

friendship with David and his defense of him in front of Saul. This discernment is herein revealed in his resolve to act. Likewise, during the reign of Jehoram, King of Israel, four lepers outside of the gate of Samaria had the same resolve when they said to one another, "Why sit we here until we die?" (2 Kings 7:3). Without spiritual gallantry, the day would not have been won. Something within Jonathan was holding the reigns. There was something within him that he could not quite explain. This God-thing within him would not let him rest. It spurred him to muster himself; it spurred him on to spiritual heroism. We now recognize this "something" as the power of the Holy Spirit. It is the move of God upon the face of the waters; the listing of the Spirit as it wills.

> *Something within me that holdeth the reins.*
> *Something within me that banishes pain;*
> *Something within me I can't explain,*
> *All that I know, there is something within me*[40]

"One of the greatest gifts God has given to you is that 'something' that is within you. That 'something' that guides and directs you. That 'something' that tells pain to stand back. That 'something' that keeps you stable in an unstable world. I can't really explain that 'something', but God has placed this 'something' within you."[41]

Jonathan was swift to hear from God and slow to speak to man. Jonathan speaks neither to his father nor to any of the other troops but to his armor-bearer alone. He speaks of a daring, unprecedented, commando-type plan to surprise the enemy. "Come, and let us go over to the Philistine's garrison, that is on the other side" (v. 1). Scripture records the command to "come" three times: (vs. 1, 6 and 12). The second time Jonathan adds a pivotal phrase: "It may be that the Lord will work for us: for there is no restraint to the Lord to save by many or by few" (v. 6).

The Message Bible gives this version: "Perhaps the Lord will help us, for nothing can hinder the Lord. He can win a battle whether he

---

[40] Sherman Haywood Cox II, *"Something Within Me."*

[41] Sherman Haywood Cox II, SoulPreaching.com

has many warriors or only a few!" And the LXX[42] renders Jonathan's declaration this way: "If peradventure the Lord may do something for us; for the Lord is not straitened to save by many or by few" (v. 6). The RSV says, "Nothing can hinder the Lord from saving by many or by few." Jonathan knew that God can do anything, but also he knew that God's doing anything was here contingent upon and was going to be a response to him doing something.

Jonathan also called the Philistines "uncircumcised, which was a term of derision often used by Israelites to designate Gentiles or enemies. However, it is also a reminder of the covenant of God with His people. Jonathan and his armor-bearer are covenant people of Yahweh; therefore, numerical odds [did] not apply, for the Lord was on their side."[43]

Do Something!

On the face of it, climbing down one side of the ravine and up the other side to confront a well-fortified enemy was a crazy idea, but Jonathan believed that God would somehow honor his act of courage. "It may be that the Lord will work for us." Jonathan's "expression did not imply a doubt; it signified simply that the object he aimed at was not in his own power—but it depended upon God—and that he expected success neither from his own strength nor on his own merit." Jonathan believed that "God is able to do exceedingly, abundantly, above all we can ask or think, according to the power that works in us" (Ephesians 3:27). Jonathan believed that "there is no restraint to the Lord." In other words, this confession of Jonathan's coincides with the declaration of the angel: "For with God nothing shall be impossible" (Luke 1:37, KJV). Likewise, our Lord encouraged the disciples when he "said unto them, 'With men this is impossible; but with God all things are possible'" (Matthew 19:26, KJV). Jonathan believed this, and so did his armor-bearer, who said, "Go

---

[42] Septuagint: The oldest Greek version of the Old Testament, traditionally said to have been translated by 70 Jewish scholars.

[43] Jack Hayford, *Spirit Filled Life Bible (Nashville: Thomas Nelson Publishers, 1991), p. 413.*

ahead. Do what you think best. I'm with you all the way" (v. 7, The Message).

To go to the other side was no small feat. Not only was Jonathan exposing himself and his confidant to the enemy, but they were exposing themselves to the rugged and dangerous elements as well. Without modern mountain climbing gear, Jonathan climbed "upon his hands and upon his feet and his armor-bearer after him" (v. 13). It actually was a rock climbing exhibition extraordinaire. "Saul formed a standing army at Michmash, 9 miles north of Jerusalem and 5 miles north of Gibeah in extremely rugged terrain. It is 1,980 feet in elevation . . . and there was an extremely deep and rugged ravine separating the two encampments. It was the most improbable route one could choose."[44] In addition to being a trained warrior, Jonathan must have been a skilled climber so he could say like David, "He makes my feet like the feet of a deer; he enables me to stand on the heights. He trains my hands for battle" (2 Sam 22:34–35, NIV).

"The Philistines had sent a detachment of soldiers to establish a new outpost to guard the pass at Michmash (13:23), and Jonathan saw this as an opportunity to attack and see the Lord work. Saul was hesitating in unbelief (14:2) while his son was acting by faith."[45] The Message Bible paints a bleak picture and casts Saul in a terrible light; "Saul was taking it easy under the pomegranate tree at the threshing floor on the edge of town at Geba (1 Samuel 14:2)." Yet here, Jonathan knew that sitting still was not the answer.

Adam Clarke states that "this action of Jonathan was totally contrary to the laws of war; no military operation should be undertaken without the knowledge and command of the general. But it is likely that he was led to this by a divine influence."[46] Eislen, Lewis, and Downey concur and portend that "to divine God's will by means of chance remarks made by the enemy (14:9) may not be a very

---

[44]   Jack W. Hayford, *Spirit Filled Life Bible* (Nashville: Thomas Nelson Publishers, 1991), pp. 412–413.

[45]   The Bible Exposition Commentary: Old Testament © 2001–2004 by Warren W. Wiersbe

[46]   Adam Clarke's Commentary, Electronic Database. Copyright © 1996, 2003, 2005, 2006 by Biblesoft.

spiritual proceeding, but it is here connected with the Hebrew conviction that the issues of all things are in the hands of God, and God is equally able to 'save by many or by few.'"[47]

Jonathan was a Godly warrior, who was "strong in the Lord and in the power of his might" (Ephesians 6:10). Jonathan relied on the power of God and not on his own strength.

> Then said Jonathan, *"Behold, we will cross over to the men, and we will show ourselves to them. If they say to us, 'Wait until we come to you,' then we will stand still in our place, and we will not go up to them.*
>
> *But if they say, 'Come up to us,' then we will go up; for the Lord has given them into our hand. And this shall be the sign to us." (1 Samuel 14:8–10, RSV)*

God Responds To Our Faith

"When Jonathan appears to prescribe a sign or token of God's will, we may infer that the same spirit which inspired this enterprise suggested the means of its execution, and put into his heart what to ask of God."[48] Jonathan knew that the weapons of his warfare were not carnal, but mighty through God" (2 Corinthians 10:4). "Jonathan was not foolhardy. He asked the Lord for a confirmation before he and his servant attacked the entire Philistine army singlehandedly."[49] And the attack by only two Hebrew soldiers was a complete surprise. "As it could not occur to the sentries that two men had come with hostile designs, it was a natural conclusion that they were

---

[47] Frederick Carl Eislen, Edwin Lewis and David G. Downey, Eds. *The Abingdon Bible Commentary*. (New York: Abington-Cokesbury Press, 1929), p. 390.

[48] Jamison-Fausset-Brown, http://jfb.biblecommenter.com/james/1.htm

[49] Morris Cerullo, *God's Victorious Army Bible* (San Diego: Morris Cerullo Word Evangelism, 1989), p. 406.

Israelite deserters. And hence no attempt was made to hinder their ascent, or stone them."[50]

Jonathan initiated a small, covert, preemptive strike. In comparison to the larger battle, this first attack may seem trivial and meaningless. In fact, the King James Version says Jonathan and his armorbearer killed "*about* 20 men," not even an exact number. "About 20" is not a large number, nor did the battle occur on a large field. It took place "within as it were about a half acre of land" (v 14). Neither was their assault known to Saul or to the greater Philistine army at the time. Yet and still, as a result of Jonathan's bold stroke, the Lord granted him strength to kill these twenty Philistines, which presumably totaled all of the soldiers in this garrison. And what follows is what stirs the soul.

Scripture tells us that immediately following Jonathan's "first slaughter," there was a "trembling in the host (of the Philistines), in the field, and among all the people; the garrison and the spoilers they also trembled, and the earth quaked: so it was a very great trembling" (v 15). God began to move! The progression of events ascends from a minor skirmish to a major, climatic conquest. We are thus reminded that "all of our battles He will fight," both great and small. God told Moses "I will be an enemy to your enemies and an adversary to your adversaries" (Exodus 23:22, RSV). Just as the hymn writer taught us, God will turn darkness into light:

> *I will make the darkness light before thee*
> *Whatever is wrong*
> *I'll make it right before thee*
> *All your battles I will fight before thee*
> *And the high places I'll bring down.*[51]

Finally, there was an earthquake. No doubt it was sent by God. Earthquakes in scripture occurred at significant junctures. Scripture records that there was an earthquake at Mt. Sinai when the law was

---

50 Jamison-Fausset-Brown Bible Commentary, http://jfb.biblecommenter. com/james/1.htm

51 Charles P. Jones, *"I Will Make The Darkness Light,"* 1916.

given and at Calvary when Jesus gave up the Ghost. Connecting the spiritual with the natural, Fausset states that "sin in the spiritual world was connected with the convulsion in the natural world. Such physical signs and premonitory upheavals shall accompany the closing conflict between the powers of light and darkness. [In this instance,] the awe it inspired made it an accompaniment attributed to Jehovah's presence."[52] Here, the conflict between two men representing all of the people of God and twenty uncircumcised Philistines was enough to cause the ground to shake. Symbolically, "in the Scriptures earthquakes are mentioned as tokens of God's power (Job 9:6) and of His presence and anger."[53]

The RSV says that "the garrison and even the raiders trembled; the earth quaked; and it became a very great panic." The literal Hebrew states that it was a trembling of God; חֶרְדָּה אֱלֹהִים, .[54] The Living Bible tells us that "Suddenly, panic broke out in the Philistine army, both in the camp and in the field, including even the outposts and raiding parties. And just then an earthquake struck, and everyone was terrified." And the NIV may say it best: "And the ground shook. It was a panic sent by God." A panic sent by God!

For no apparent reason, yet because this was Jonathan's season, panic set in and spread throughout the enemy camp. Later in chapter, 14 we read that Jonathan tasted wild honey, his eyes were opened, and he was enlightened. Even before the honey incident, Jonathan was stirred to action, was given a plan of action, and was brave enough to move with all diligent speed to carry out the action plan of God: "Behold, I have given you authority to tread upon serpents and scorpions, and over all the power of the enemy" (Luke 10:19–20, RSV). And God honored his fearless fortitude.

The lone act of faith by Jonathan was rewarded by heaven and earth took note. The earthquake, a token of God's power, was not

52   International Standard Bible Encyclopaedia, Electronic Database. Copyright © 1996, 2003, 2006 by Biblesoft, Inc.

53   International Standard Bible Commentary.

54   Biblesoft's New Exhaustive Strong's Numbers and Concordance with Expanded Greek-Hebrew Dictionary. Copyright © 1994, 2003, 2006 Biblesoft, Inc. and International Bible Translators, Inc.

understood by the enemy and panic set in. Terror struck the proud and physical Philistines, and they commenced to turn on each other. "And the watchmen of Saul in Gibeah of Benjamin looked; and, behold, the multitude melted away, and they went on beating down one another" (1 Samuel 14:16, KJV). The New Living Translation tells us that

> *while Saul was talking to the priest, the confusion in the Philistine camp grew louder and louder. So Saul said to the priest, "Never mind; let's get going!" Then Saul and all his men rushed out to the battle and found the Philistines killing each other.*
>
> *There was terrible confusion everywhere. Even the Hebrews who had previously gone over to the Philistine army revolted and joined in with Saul, Jonathan, and the rest of the Israelites. (1 Samuel 14:19–22, New Living Translation)*

For the Hebrews, things got better and better. For the Philistines, things got worse and worse. Not only did Jonathan win that first battle, but panic invaded the enemy camp so that they began to fight among themselves. And then they went on to kill each other. Further, scripture itself seems to marvel at what happened by saying that *even* the Hebrews who had previously gone over to the Philistine army revolted and joined with Saul, Jonathan, and the rest of the Israelites; thus, even the backsliding soldiers came home. Jonathan's valiant effort saved the people, and then, sadly, because of his father's foolish oath, the people had to save Jonathan.

Jonathan's divinely orchestrated upset victory was as miraculous as they come. God turned what seemed like a small, insignificant trickle into a mighty, rushing stream. The decision to "go over to the other side" was a lone, bold stroke. This was a single soldier and his singular triumphant act. Jonathan was "lone" but he was not alone: God was with him. Jonathan embarked on an impossible mission with only the confidence that "if God be for us, who can be against us?" (Romans 8:31, KJV). He proved the Scripture true: "The wicked flee when no one pursues, but the righteous are bold as a lion" (Proverbs 28:1).

Jonathan's triumph honored the Lord as the victory was wrought by God and God alone. It was not motivated by strife or vainglory. Jonathan was not puffed up or trying to show off. Jonathan wisely chose to keep the mission a secret, and God, who sees in secret, rewarded him openly (Matthew 6:6). Jonathan climbed up the side of a mountain and reached the top. The upset victory was worth the effort. His faith shook heaven and earth, and ours can too.

> *Climbing up the mountain, trying to reach the top;*
> *Almost finished my battle, gone halfway and I just*
> *can't stop;*
> *At the end of the mountain there is faith and trust.*
> *I can see Jesus standing there to meet us,*
> *I thank God, I'm reaching for myself.*[55]

Spiritual Lessons
1. God can empower and embolden any humble vessel to defeat the enemy. (Genesis 14:2)
2. God rewards faith. (Genesis 14: 6; Hebrews 11:2)
3. Change requires a decision, determination, and direction from God. (Genesis 14:2, 6, 14)
4. God can intervene and turn defeat into victory in miraculous ways. (Genesis 14:15)
5. God can do anything but fail. (Genesis 14:6)

---

[55] Mattie Moss Clark, "Climbing Up the Mountain" 1970.

CHAPTER 3

Ruth Rises to Redemption

She said to them, "Do not call me Naomi (sweetness); call me Mara (bitter), for the Almighty has caused me great grief and bitterness. I left full [with a husband and two sons], but the Lord has brought me back empty. Why call me Naomi, since the Lord has testified against me and the Almighty has afflicted me?"

So Naomi returned from the country of Moab, and with her Ruth the Moabitess, her daughter-in-law. And they arrived in Bethlehem at the beginning of the barley harvest.

Now Naomi had a relative of her husband, a man of great wealth and influence, from the family of Elimelech, whose name was Boaz. And Ruth the Moabitess said to Naomi, "Please let me go to the field and glean among the ears of grain after one [of the reapers] in whose sight I may find favor."

—Ruth 1:20–2:2, Amplified

Rudy vs. Notre Dame

They told him it couldn't be done. They told him it would never happen. In the classic, must-see film bearing his name, Rudy's father kicks dirt on the fire of his dream. "Chasing a stupid dream causes you and everyone around you heartache. Notre Dame is for rich kids; smart kids; great athletes; it's not for us!"[56] Rudy's direct response to the admissions counselor, and by extension, to his father, is this: "Ever since I was a kid I wanted to go to school (at Notre Dame). And ever since I was a kid everyone said it couldn't be done. My whole life people have told me what I could do and couldn't do. I've always listened to them, believing what they said. I don't want to do that anymore."[57] And he didn't.

"On November 8, 1975, Daniel "Rudy" Ruettiger, on the final play of the last home game of the season, sacked the Georgia Tech quarterback, and after an uproar went up from the crowd and smiles went across the faces around the stadium, including his father's, Rudy was lifted onto the shoulders of his teammates and carried off the field."[58] Ruth, like Rudy, experienced one setback after another in her quest to live her dream. For Ruth, it seemed as if everything and everyone was against her. She was a barren Moabite widow. She wasn't rich, she wasn't book-smart, and she wasn't great. Yet she stuck to Naomi, her mother-in-law, and humbled herself to do menial tasks. True to scripture, in due time, God exalted her. She learned that she was related to Boaz who became her kinsman redeemer. She married Boaz and gave birth to Obed, the father of Jesse, the father of David. If they could, these favorite sons would have lifted Ruth onto their shoulders and carried her off the spiritual playing field. Her dream, her longing to bear a son, was fulfilled. And she not only bore a son, but she winnowed her way into the first family of the household of God and became an ancestress of Jesus Christ.

---

56   *"Rudy,"* The film, 1993.

57   Ibid.

58   http://bleacherreport.com/articles/328263-the-true-story-of-notre-dames-famous-walk-on-daniel-rudy-reutigger

To our generation, Ruth is a female Rudy and her story is an implausible upset victory, a compelling comeback, a total turnaround. "Ruth was poor, a foreigner, and a woman, and all this counted against her, but she was helped by an older woman to overcome the difficulties she faced. She had the good sense to listen to the advice given to her by Naomi, and the older woman was rewarded by Ruth's unfaltering loyalty. Her story illustrates the triumph of courage and ingenuity over adverse circumstances. She has special significance for Christians: in the gospel of Matthew, four women appear in the genealogy of Jesus (Matthew 1:2–17), and Ruth was one of the four."[59]

The central figure in Ruth's life was Naomi who moved with her husband and sons from Bethlehem to Moab and lived there ten years. "The land of Moab is named after the eldest son of Lot, the incestuous offspring of Lot's older daughter, near Zoar, southeast of the Dead Sea (Genesis 19:37)."[60] Another commentator states that "Moab was a region northeast of the Dead Sea. The Moabites, descendants of Lot, worshiped Chemosh and other pagan gods. Scripture records two times when they fought against Israel (Judges 3:12–30 and I Samuel 14:47)."[61] Moab's sordid history includes "refusing Israel's request for passage through Edom and Moab and liberty to purchase bread and water"[62] (Judges 11:17; Numbers 20:14–21). Further, "the daughters of Moab, mentioned in Numbers 25:1, were those with whom Israel 'began whoredom.'"[63] This bleak backdrop, notwithstanding, Ruth rises from the ruinous refuse of Moab's past and emerges as one of the shining stars of God's grace.

Naomi came home with next to nothing. Yet her coming home was a comeback of epic proportions. She left Bethlehem with her

---

[59] http://www.womeninthebible.net/1.13.Ruth.htm

[60] Fausset's Bible Dictionary, Electronic Database Copyright © 1998, 2003, 2006 by Biblesoft, Inc.

[61] Kenneth D. Boa, Ed., *The New Open Bible Study Edition,* (Nashville: Thomas Nelson Publishers), p. 316.

[62] Fausset's Bible Dictionary, Electronic Database Copyright © 1998, 2003, 2006 by Biblesoft, Inc.

[63] Ibid.

husband and two sons. She left because of a famine during the time the judges ruled. Theologically speaking, "famine is a sign of disobedience and apostasy" and the period of the judges "was a time of apostasy, warfare, decline, violence, moral decay and anarchy."[64] Naomi left her home, her heritage, and her inheritance. She left all with her husband for Moab—the land of the enemy of Israel. And in Moab, things went from bad to worse. In Moab she lost her husband, Elimelech, and her two sons, Mahlon and Chilion. First her husband died, and then her married sons died. So after about ten years, Naomi, a widow with no sons and no grandsons, decided to return home.

Her daughters-in-law, Orpah and Ruth, wanted to return to the land of promise with her, but she begs them not to and tries to convince them otherwise. Orpah puts up a fight, but yields to her mother-in-law. Ruth, on the other hand, refuses to leave Naomi and commits to stay with her until death. Ruth's confession to Naomi is one for the ages:

Teammates: *Ruth and Naomi*

> But Ruth said, "Entreat me not to leave you or to return from following you; for where you go I will go, and where you lodge I will lodge; your people shall be my people, and your God my God; where you die I will die, and there will I be buried.
>
> May the Lord do so to me and more also if even death parts me from you." And when Na'omi saw that she was determined to go with her, she said no more. (Ruth 1:16–18, RSV)

"The totality of this commitment is emphasized by its terseness (merely four words in the Hebrew: 'amekh 'ami we'lohaikh 'elohai, which literally means 'your people my people; your God my God'). Yet Ruth extended her commitment still further, beyond death itself:

---

[64] Kenneth D. Boa, Ed., *The New Open Bible Study Edition*, (Nashville: Thomas Nelson Publishers), p. 317.

'Where you die I will die, and there I will be buried' (verse 17) . . . The location of burial [was significant because it] was important to them . . . Ruth was willing to forgo everything —her future in Moab, her people, her gods and even her ancestral burial plot—to be joined with Naomi."[65]

When Naomi saw that Ruth could not be dissuaded, she stopped arguing and the two traveled back to Bethlehem together. Cheerful for the companionship but cynical about her circumstances, Naomi arrives home with next to nothing, nothing except her daughter-in-law who was a Moabite.

Upon arriving in Bethlehem, everyone was excited to see her after so long an absence. But Naomi was less than enthused about being home. She was emotionally bruised, bitter, battered, and broken; and she blamed God for it. She went from disappointment to discouragement to dare we say depression as the root of bitterness had set in and taken hold. Instead of being thankful to be back in the land of promise and in Bethlehem, the house of Bread, she launches a tirade directed at God. Her words are acrid and acidic and laced with verbal cyanide:

> *And she said unto them, Call me not Naomi, call me Mara: for the Almighty hath dealt very bitterly with me. I went out full, and the Lord hath brought me home again empty: why then call ye me Naomi, seeing the Lord hath testified against me, and the Almighty hath afflicted me? (Ruth 1:20–21, KJV)*

From Bitter To Better

Emotionally and theologically, Naomi is about as low as you can go. She said and believed that the Lord had afflicted and "testified against" her. In essence, she alleges that God has turned his back on her. Her hope was in her husband, but he died. Her help was in her two sons, but they died too. All had abandoned her, all except for Ruth. But what could she do? "Naomi reflects human nature in gen-

---

[65] http://www.gci.org/bible/hist/ruth2

eral as she blames God, rather than personal choices and sin nature, for the destructive and painful things she is experiencing. Naomi's behavior is characteristic of a person outside of the covenant; thus she inappropriately indicates her circumstances to be the result of God's punitive action."[66] The truth was, the traditional decision-making process was the husbands, and in this instance, death followed for her husband and her sons—all the men in her life.

At the end of Ruth chapter 1, the contrast between Naomi and Ruth couldn't be more extreme. Ruth, the gentile, became a proselyte. Naomi, the child of promise, seemingly loses her faith and confidence in God. Ruth pledges her life to Naomi and her God; Naomi testifies that "the hand of the Lord has gone out against me" (1:13). "Ruth is a virtuous woman (3:11) who shows loyal love to her mother-in-law,"[67] hence, Ruth is a moral woman, yet Naomi's morale is failing. Naomi grieves that everything is lost, while Ruth, coming from Moab to Israel, sees that she has everything to gain.

"Yet as we remember Ruth, as we acknowledge and strive to emulate her devotion, her loyalty, her total commitment, let us not forget that other remarkable woman, Naomi. As F.B. Huey, Jr., explains, 'Naomi's consistent living must have so impressed her daughter-in-law to cause her to abandon her homeland and her gods.' "[68] What sort of woman was this Naomi, to inspire such affection in a daughter-in-law? What relationship with God must she have had to cause Ruth to forsake the gods of Moab and worship Naomi's God alone?"[69]

It seems that Naomi saved Ruth from Moab, and Ruth in turn saves Naomi from misery and misfortune. It is evident that "God loved Ruth and Naomi. He knew what was going on in their lives. Ruth's relationship with God started the same way most relationships with Him do. She came to know and value someone who knew Him

---

[66]   Jack W. Hayford, *Spirit Filled Life Bible* (Nashville: Thomas Nelson Publishers, 1991), p. 389.

[67]   Kenneth D. Boa, Ed., *The New Open Bible Study Edition,* (Nashville: Thomas Nelson Publishers), p. 317.

[68]   'Ruth," in The Expositor's Bible Commentary, vol. 3, p. 524).

[69]   http://www.gci.org/bible/hist/ruth2

well. That someone was Naomi. These women were not only God's provision to each other but also a way for Him to make Himself known through their lives."[70]

Naomi's shortsighted faith failed to see beyond her current state. At least one expositor claims that Naomi "never stopped trusting [God] to do something about her situation."[71] Not so! There are times when we in our human frailty stop trusting God even if for a moment or day or season. Naomi lies before us as an example of this negativity. Naomi blames God for her situation, and to show how far she has fallen, she changes her name from Naomi, which means "pleasant" to "Mara," meaning bitter. "A great deal may be in a name, especially a name one chooses to live up to. Naomi calls herself Mara, and she blamed God for it.

It is well to remember that at the period in which the story is set, God was considered to be the author of all actions and events, good and bad."[72] This theology, of course, is flawed. "Naomi chose to look at the worst side of life when she asked to be called Mara . . . and she did not realize that to trust God when we have every reason for distrusting him is the supreme triumph of religion."[73]

The author of the great hymn "Great Is Thy Faithfulness" wrote that God is our "strength for today" and our "bright hope for tomorrow." Despite the rigors of the day, regardless of the darkness of the night, God is our strength and hope. "The book of Ruth is a study in the sovereignty of God, emphasizing the sustaining mercy of God, which brings a fruitful end of a story that begins with famine, death and loss."[74]

---

[70] http://bible.org/seriespage/lesson-5-naomi-and-ruth-mothers-and-daughters

[71] http://www.gci.org/bible/hist/ruth2

[72] George Arthur Buttrick, *The Interpreters Bible, Volume 2.* (Nashville: Abingdon Press), 1991, p. 838.

[73] Ibid.

[74] Jack W. Hayford, *Spirit Filled Life Bible* (Nashville: Thomas Nelson Publishers). 1991, p. 385.

The Comeback Starts Now!

The Book of Ruth is a four-part harmony. At the close of the first stanza, the staggering, despairing events leading up to Naomi's return are met with a glimmer of hope that peaks over the horizon. The last verse of chapter 1 signals the beginning of her spiritual comeback. In her darkest hour, unbeknownst to her, God was there. Even though she didn't know it, Naomi was about to experience a brand-new beginning. Beginnings are symbolic of births, and new beginnings are figurative of the new birth. As Naomi returned from Moab to Bethlehem with Ruth, her hymn of praise could have been

> *Summer and winter, and springtime and harvest,*
> *Sun, moon and stars in their courses above,*
> *Join with all nature in manifold witness*
> *To Thy great faithfulness, mercy and love.*[75]

In the providence of God, she arrived home just in time. Naomi's comeback was tied to Ruth and to the beginning of the barley harvest. Note that it was the "beginning" of the barley harvest. It was not the middle or the end. She did not come too early or arrive too late. She did not miss her harvest! She arrived home to a fresh start and renewed hope—for God is the author of all new beginnings.

It is ironic to note that harvest is not a start, but an end, the end of the growing season. It is the time when ripened crops are gathered. This harvest was the end of Naomi's struggle and misery and the beginning of her return and restoration. It was the end of Ruth's life as an alien and the beginning of her adoption and acceptance into the household of faith.

Harvest time is a time of joy and gladness. Harvest time is a time of singing and dancing and rejoicing. The end of the growing season signaled the beginning of the gathering season; it was a time of celebration.

---

[75] Thomas Obediah Chisholm, v. 2, *"Great is Thy Faithfulness."*

And we shall come rejoicing, bringing in the sheaves.[76]

God delights in fixing it so that we celebrate even when it appears we should throw in the towel. The darkest hour is just before the day. And oft-times we defend defeat when instead we should be vying for victory. Likewise, when Naomi returned to Bethlehem, she was not in the praising mood. God indeed had been faithful to Naomi, but she couldn't see over the horizon. All she had was the companionship of one daughter-in-law, Ruth. Naomi had no husband, no sons and seemingly, no future. Fortunately for Naomi, the words of the prophet Jeremiah did not apply to her:

> *The harvest is past, the summer is ended and we are not saved. (Jeremiah 8:20, RSV)*

Bitter and depressed, Naomi is on her way to one of the greatest comebacks in biblical history. Comebacks are thrilling because of their improbability and unexpected, illogical consummation. In every comeback victory in life, and in all situations that God turns around, there is a point in time when the comeback begins that can hardly be traced, but it exists nonetheless. In Naomi's case, the comeback was the divine timing of her return. Her comeback was underway and she didn't even know it. God was orchestrating events, especially the attachment of Ruth, which would play into the history of redemption. "Naomi's misfortune leads her to think that God is her enemy, yet He has plans she does not yet realize."[77]

Take Your Eyes Off Of The Problem

Naomi's fortune began to turn before she did. Yet turn she did. Naomi turned her attention from her suffering to the needs of Ruth, her companion and friend. It is no coincidence that the name Ruth indeed means friend. People can be as fickle as the weather. Friends can change their countenance toward you as quickly as a late-after-

---

76 Knowles Shaw, *"Bringing in the Sheaves,"* 1874.
77 Kenneth D. Boa, Ed., *The New Open Bible Study Edition.* (Nashville: Thomas Nelson Publishers), p. 317.

noon storm changes the face of a summer sky. But God is not fickle nor does he change. God told the prophet Malachi, "I am the Lord, I change not" (Malachi 3:6, KJV). Through Ruth, God proved that he will come alongside and be our helper in the time of storm. Ruth proved that "a friend loveth at all times" (Proverbs 17:17). In her darkest hour, unbeknownst to her, God was there, working behind the scenes.

Once Naomi took her eyes off herself and her situation and focused on someone other than herself, she saw the hand of God at work on her behalf. Not only was it the beginning of the barley harvest, but there was a near kinsman of her husband's that she knew not of. Ruth 2:1 tells us

> *Now Na'omi had a kinsman of her husband's, a man of wealth, of the family of Elim'elech, whose name was Bo'az. (Ruth 2:1)*

God's provision of a kinsman redeemer was huge. It was Naomi and Ruth's saving grace. Without a redeemer, they were bound to a life of begging and pleading and scrimping and scraping. "If a man died in Bible times, his widow often suffered at the hands of the powerful (Job 24:21). This was especially true if she had no family to provide for her and her children."[78]

Indeed, then and now, God has always been concerned about the plight of the widow (Ps 68:5; 146:9). Through the Mosaic Law, God provided her with the opportunity to glean in the fields, orchards, and vineyards after the harvesters had taken most of the crop (Deuteronomy 24:19–22)."[79] Further, the "law of the [Kinsman-Redeemer] helped to protect the poor from being exploited and the rich from taking property from one tribe to another. The redeemer had to be a near kinsman who was able to redeem and willing to

---

[78] Nelson's Student Bible Commentary, *"Widow"* (Nashville: Thomas Nelson, 2005), p. 265.

[79] Nelson's Illustrated Bible Dictionary, *"Leah"*, Copyright © 1986, Thomas Nelson Publishers.

redeem. He was not obligated to do so, but it was expected of him. To refuse was to hurt the family and tribe as well as his own reputation"[80]

In Ruth, God saw fit not only to give us a story filled with the faithfulness, companionship, and devotion of a daughter-in-law to her mother-in-law, but He also gave us a love story between a prominent, wealthy Jewish landowner and a poor, barren Moabite widow. "Boaz is described as a *gibbor chayil,* a phrase which can mean either 'a mighty man of valor' or else 'a man of position and wealth.' The latter is probably the sense in which the phrase is applied to Boaz."[81]

Without the knowledge that she had married into a nation that held to the law of the kinsmen redeemer, nor the knowledge that Boaz owned fields in Bethlehem, at the beginning of chapter 2, Ruth takes the initiative. Something in Ruth told her that she needed to take action now. She says to Naomi

> *And Ruth the Moabitess said unto Naomi, Let me*
> *now go to the field, and glean ears of corn after him*
> *in whose sight I shall find grace. (Ruth 2:2, KJV)*

Once again, another faith-filled follower of God understood the eternal "now" of God. Ruth said, I need to go the field now. I can't wait another minute or another moment. I need to go now. Why? Because now is the arrival time of God. Now is the accepted time. Now is the right time. Now is the correct time. The apostle Paul exhorted,

> *Behold, now is the accepted time; behold, now is the*
> *day of salvation. (2 Corinthians 6:2, KJV)*

Get Going!

Ruth said I will go to the field now. These are words of faith indeed. Ruth committed to go to the field and glean, to scrimp and scrape leftover crops in order to eat and provide for her mother-in-

---

[80]   W.W. Wiersbe, *With the Word,* pg. 157.

[81]   International Standard Bible Encyclopaedia, *"Leah,"* Electronic Database Copyright © 1996, 2003, 2006 by Biblesoft, Inc.

law. Ruth's ruggedness teaches us that not every victory is a blowout. Some wins are eked out. On her way to a thrilling victory, Ruth was willing to perform unheralded, menial tasks. To live by faith means to take God at His word and then act upon it, for "faith without works is dead" (James 2:20, NKJV).

Since Ruth believed in the God of her mother-in-law, she trusted that God would provide for them both. So she set out to find a field in which she could glean. This was completely an act of faith because, being a stranger, she didn't know who owned the various parcels of ground that made up the fields. There were boundary markers for each parcel, but no fences or family name signs as seen on our farms today. Furthermore, as a woman and an outsider, she was especially vulnerable; and she had to be careful where she went."[82]

The combination of the "going" of Ruth and the "coming" of Boaz was the hand of God at work. Ruth says, "Let me now go" (Ruth 2:2, KJV), and then we read, "and behold, Boaz came" (Ruth 2:4, KJV). Going and coming; coming and going. Only God can time the routine movements of life to benefit those whose heart hungers for him! To further emphasize the importance of divine intervention, the LXX states that "she happened by chance to come on a portion of the land of Booz (Ruth 2:3)." The KJV says that "and her hap was to light on a part of the field belonging unto Boaz, who was of the kindred of Elimelech." The NIV may say it best: "As it turned out, she found herself working in a field belonging to Boaz."

Ruth turned to God, and God turned to Ruth. And so did things. And we believe that "things will turn out" for us as well. Children of faith who have been grafted into the covenant of promise know that in God's economy, nothing is by accident or by happenstance. All is used and no incident is a coincidence. By faithfully following Naomi, Ruth sought the favor of God and, in so doing, found favor in the eyes of Boaz.

Here is another one of those "boy meets girl" stories, but this time, it's God's version. First, Boaz took knowledge of her, just as the angel of the Lord took knowledge of Hagar. The phrase "that thou

---

[82] The Bible Exposition Commentary: Old Testament © 2001–2004 by Warren W. Wiersbe.

shouldest take knowledge of me" (Ruth 2:10, KJV), this should be the Hebrew word rk^n* nakar (naw-kar'), which is a primitive root and means to scrutinize, i.e., look intently at; hence (with recognition implied), to acknowledge; be acquainted with; care for, respect, revere."[83] God takes knowledge of us, especially when we are tired, weary, and worn. "The eyes of the Lord are upon the righteous, and his ears are open unto their cry" (Psalm 34:15, KJV). Noah lived among a faithless and perverse nation. "But Noah found favor in the eyes of the Lord" (Genesis 6:8, RSV). Noah was righteous and faithful, and it appears that Ruth was too.

Boaz took one look at Ruth, and he was smitten. He inquired of her and found out who she was, and whose she was. When he learned that she belonged to his now-deceased relative Elimelech, he was motivated even the more to take action. Because of this and his fondness of her, he showed her grace and favor. "For the grace of God has appeared, bringing salvation to all men" (Titus 2:11–12, NASB). The grace of God brought us salvation, and it is herein foreshadowed how God would adopt the gentiles and bring them into his family. Ruth called herself "a stranger." We are thus reminded of the words of the great hymn:

> *Jesus sought me when a stranger,*
> *wandering from the fold of God.*
> *He to rescue me from danger,*
> *interposed His precious blood.*[84]

Boaz prophesied to Ruth that she would be rewarded. "May the Lord reward your work, and your wages be full from the Lord, the God of Israel, under whose wings you have come to seek refuge" (v. 12, NASB). The KJV says that Boaz decreed not only a reward, but he prophesied that she would receive "a full reward." Ruth's humility and devotion shined as she expressed gratitude to Boaz. She said, "I have found favor in your sight, my lord, for you have comforted me

---

[83] Biblesoft's New Exhaustive Strong's Numbers and Concordance with Expanded Greek-Hebrew Dictionary, Copyright © 1994, 2003, 2006.

[84] Robert Robinson, *"Come thou Fount of Every Blessing," v. 2,* 1758.

and indeed have spoken kindly to your maidservant, though I am not like one of your maidservants" (v. 13, NASB).

Grace Must Be Found

Ruth found grace in the eyes of the Lord, and in the gaze of Boaz. Further proof is that Boaz ordered his workers to "purposely pull out for her some grain from the bundles and leave it [on the ground]," especially for Ruth. The KJV uses the phrase "handfuls of purpose" (v. 16). Thus, her gleaning was made easy. Even as we persevere through trials, Jesus said that his "yoke is easy" his "burden is light" (Matthew 11:30).

Ruth went home with almost more than she could carry. Naomi was so enlightened that she immediately began to make plans for her future. Wedding plans. The story winds through the perseverance of Boaz in his effort to redeem her, paralleling our Lord's efforts to restore and redeem lost mankind.

All the world loves a happy ending. This story ends with Boaz redeeming Ruth by marrying her, thus fulfilling his obligation to her dead husband as a kinsman redeemer. At the end of chapter 4, Ruth was blessed to bare a son, and she called his name Obed. And Obed begat Jessie, and Jessie begat David (4:17). Ruth came out of nowhere and burst onto the scene to become the great-grandmother of David. How unthinkable only a few short chapters before! And when God pulls off such an upset, such a comeback, such a turnaround as this, everyone will know it! The women of Bethlehem joined the chorus in saying:

> *Blessed be the Lord, which hath not left thee this day without a kinsman, that his name may be famous in Israel. And he shall be unto thee a restorer of thy life, and a nourisher of thine old age: for thy daughter in law, which loveth thee, which is better to thee than seven sons, hath born him. (Ruth 4:14–15, KJV)*

Ruth was like us, and we are like Ruth. We were "Gentiles in the flesh, called 'Uncircumcision' by the so-called 'Circumcision,' which is performed in the flesh . . . separate from Christ, excluded from the commonwealth of Israel, and strangers to the covenants of promise, having no hope and without God in the world" (Ephesians 2:11–12, NASB). Ruth was without hope, and so were we. Ruth was a Gentile, and so were we. Ruth was excluded from the Commonwealth of Israel, and so were we. Ruth was a stranger to the covenant of promise, and so were we. But grace came! "For by grace are ye saved through faith; and that not of yourselves: it is the gift of God" (Ephesians 2:8, KJV). Grace came for Ruth and grace has come for us! God's Amazing Grace!

Undeserved and unexpected, grace came. It came with a loving mother-in-law. It came at the beginning of the barley harvest. It came at the field of Boaz. It came in the person of Boaz. It came when she sat beside the reapers. It came with handfuls of purpose. It came with an overflow of grain. It came with marriage to Boaz and birth to a man child named Obed. Grace came! Famine couldn't stop it. Death couldn't stop it. Depression couldn't stop it. Defeat couldn't stop it. Nothing can stop grace! And as we remain faithful to God and to those near us, grace will find us and save us, grace will bring us from all the way back, and grace will turn all things around for our good.

> *Wonderful grace of Jesus,*
> *Greater than all my sin;*
> *How shall my tongue describe it,*
> *where shall its praise begin?*
> *Taking away my burden,*
> *setting my spirit free,*
> *For the wonderful grace of Jesus*
> *reaches me.*[85]

---

[85] Haldor Lillenas. *"Wonderful Grace of Jesus."* 1918.

Spiritual Lessons from Ruth

1. God's timing is always perfect. (Ruth 1:29)
2. God always has a plan. (Ruth 2:1)
3. God will reward faith and faithfulness with favor and provision that is more than enough.
4. God delights in surprising us with unexpected blessings. (Ruth 2:31)
5. God sent his Son to earth, and "by being born at Bethlehem, Jesus Christ became our near kinsman. He was able to save and willing to save; He saves all who will put their trust in Him."[86]

---

[86] W.W. Wiersbe, *With the Word,* p. 157.

CHAPTER 4

Moses's Mountain Miracle

Now Amalek came and fought with Israel in Rephidim. And Moses said to Joshua, "Choose us some men and go out, fight with Amalek. Tomorrow I will stand on the top of the hill with the rod of God in my hand."

So Joshua did as Moses said to him, and fought with Amalek. And Moses, Aaron, and Hur went up to the top of the hill. And so it was, when Moses held up his hand, that Israel prevailed; and when he let down his hand, Amalek prevailed.

—Exodus 17:8–11, NKJV

The Boston Red Sox Find Redemption

"When the night of October 16, 2004, came to a merciful end, the Curse of the Bambino was alive and well. The New York Yankees, led by A-Rod, Jeter, and Sheffield, had just extended their ALCS lead to three games to none over the Boston Red Sox, and seemed on course to yet another trip to the World Series. But the cold October winds of change began to blow. Over four consecutive days and nights, this determined Red Sox team miraculously won four straight games to overcome their past and chart a new destiny."[87] For baseball fans in general, and for "Red Sox Nation" in particular, the Red Sox come-from-behind victory over their archrival, the New York Yankees, was cause for euphoria; down 0-3, a comeback was unthinkable.

The "Amazing Red Sox went on to win the World Series to end 86 years of frustration with a sweep of the St. Louis Cardinals."[88] The headline on the cover of the *Boston Globe* was a simple "YES!!!" Likewise, the fledgling nation of Israel's defeat of the heavily armed and fierce Amalekite force was similarly unexplainable, humanly speaking. As the fight wore on, alarmingly, the balance of the battle began to slip and tipped in the enemies favor. Yet when the battle was not going their way, Moses lifted and stretched his hands toward heaven, and everything turned around. Israel overcame their past and charted a new destiny.

Israel vs. the Amalekites

Exodus 17 records a dramatic battle between Israel and the Amalekites. It is the first battle with another foe after the Exodus. After 430 years of slavery, Israel first had to shed her self-imposed slave mentality and adopt her new, God-given national identity. Israel had to learn how to fight. Israel, as well as we, must heed the hymn writer's call:

> *Fight the good fight with all thy might;*
> *Christ is thy Strength, and Christ thy right;*
> *Lay hold on life, and it shall be*
> *Thy joy and crown eternally.*[89]

En route out of Egypt, they first had to battle thirst. Battling thirst is one thing; battling a physical foe is another. Yet water was supernaturally provided when Moses struck the rock at God's com-

---

[87] *"30 For 30: Four Days in October,"* Major League Baseball Productions, 2010.

[88] *The Boston Globe*, Thursday, October 28, 2004.

[89] John S. B. Monsell, *"Fight The Good Fight With All Thy Might,"* 1863.

mand. Then God further proved Himself to Israel as He supernaturally provided an upset victory.

An Unfair Fight

As Moses and the children of Israel marched from their Red Sea victory over their Egyptian oppressors toward Mt. Sinai, they were attacked. Not only were the children of Israel attacked; they were attached *from behind*. Some fell behind and the Amalekites came up from behind. The unprovoked sneak attack targeted the weak, the weary and the worn among God's people; the elderly, women and children, and those who just couldn't keep up who took up the rear of the progression. "It does not appear that the Israelites gave them any kind of provocation, they seem to have attacked them merely through the hopes of plunder."[90]

Moses led the massive march from the point where the Israelites crossed the Red Sea en route to Mt. Sinai, and Amalek met them somewhere in between. That's generally how the enemy operates. He tries to catch us when our anxiety is high and our resistance is low. Our adversary attacks our faintness, our feebleness, and our flimsiness. Our fierce foe doesn't fight fair, as he hits below the belt when we are weary, weak, and worn. Our enemy tries to pin us down, and somewhere between here and there, he tries to hem us in.

The baby nation was taking baby steps and was teetering like a toddler learning how to walk. They weren't where they had been, but they hadn't quite yet arrived at where they were going. They were no longer in Egypt, but their destination, the Promised Land, was no way near either; they were somewhere between the prophesy and the promise. "On Israel's route from Egypt to Palestine, Amalek in guerrilla warfare tried to stop their progress . . . It was a deliberate effort to defeat God's purpose at the very outset, while Israel was as yet feeble, having just come out of Egypt. The motive is stated expressly, 'Amalek feared not God.'"[91]

---

[90] Adam Clarke's Commentary, Electronic Database. Copyright © 1996, 2003, 2005, 2006 by Biblesoft, Inc.

[91] Fausset's Bible Dictionary, *"AMALEKITES,"* Electronic Database Copyright © 1998, 2003, 2006 by Biblesoft, Inc.

Thus, the battle was a spiritual war from the start. These enemies of Israel were first the enemies of God, for they had "no fear of God" (Deuteronomy 25:18). The Hebrews were commanded to fear the Lord, and the Amalekites were like the wicked judge of Luke 18; they feared not God, nor regarded man. The Amalekites approached from behind and performed "a wicked deed, slaughtering the old people and the children, the pregnant and the sick which could not move quite as fast as the rest of the progression."[92]

In contrast to the victory against Pharaoh where the Lord fought for them and they held their peace, in this battle, Moses and the Israelites were forced to fight. According to Barnes, "The attack occurred about two months after the Exodus, toward the end of May or early in June, when the Bedouins leave the lower plains in order to find pasture for their flocks on the cooler heights."[93] The Amalekites very name means warlike. They were a fierce roaming band of land pirates looking to raid any all that crossed their path. What the Amalekites did was so heinous, so cruel, and so sinister that God commanded Moses to order their complete annihilation once the Israelites were settled into the Promised Land. "The crime of Amalek is more fully described in Deuteronomy 25:17–19:

> *Remember what Amalek did unto thee by the way,*
> *when ye were come forth out of Egypt; How he met*
> *thee by the way, and smote the hindmost of thee,*
> *even all that were feeble behind thee, when thou*
> *wast faint and weary; and he feared not God.*
> *Therefore it shall be, when the Lord thy God hath*
> *given thee rest from all thine enemies round about,*
> *in the land which the Lord thy God giveth thee for*
> *an inheritance to possess it, that thou shalt blot out*
> *the remembrance of Amalek from under heaven;*
> *thou shalt not forget it.*

---

92 Jamie Buckingham, *A Way Through the Wilderness* (Old Tapan, New Jersey: Chosen Books) 1986, p. 106.

93 Barnes' Notes, Electronic Database Copyright © 1997, 2003, 2005, 2006 by Biblesoft, Inc.

Blessed Are The Underdogs

Statistically speaking, the Amalekites had the edge because of their years of fighting experience, their fierce nature, and their historical anger. According to some historians, Amalek was the grandson of Esau, who sold his birthright and lost his blessing to his younger brother Jacob whose name was changed to Israel. Amalek was and his name means "warlike." They represented more than a warring tribe . . . but that entire breed of people who are the enemies of God and enemies of God's people . . . They had no regard for the sanctity of human life, no morals, no sense of ethics . . . The prophet Balaam described the Amalekites as 'the first fruits of the heathen,' or the beginning of all those races of the people hostile toward the people of God."[94]

It seems as if this was the first of many future battles between the sons of Abraham and Isaac, between Arab and Jew. However, at least one other source states that "they are not to be identified with the descendants of Esau (Genesis 36:12, 16) because they are mentioned earlier, in the account of the invasion of Chedorlaomer (Genesis 14:7) and in Balaam's prophecy (Numbers 24:20), Amalek is called 'the first of the nations,' which seems to refer to an early existence. We are uncertain of their origin, for they do not appear in the list of nations found in Genesis 10. They do not seem to have had any relationship with the tribes of Israel, save as, we may surmise, some of the descendants of Esau were incorporated into the tribe."[95]

Physically, Israel didn't stand a chance against these well-trained marauders. However, since this wasn't a physical fight, God gave Moses supernatural insight, and God gave him clear instruction. The new nation had a new captain, Joshua, Moses's minister, who would lead the fight while Moses accepted a new role of commander in chief and overseer. "Joshua is here represented without introduction

---

[94] Ibid., p. 107.

[95] International Standard Bible Encyclopaedia, Electronic Database Copyright © 1996, 2003, 2006 by Biblesoft, Inc.

as chief warrior. In Exodus 33:11 he is represented as Moses' personal servant, a 'young man.'"[96]

While Moses led a formidable force of males, some six hundred thousand strong, only choice men were singled out to defend Israel. He told Joshua to "choose for us men" (v. 9). Even with hand-picked men chosen to fight, this band of brothers had never fought together before, at least not like this. We are thus reminded that even as God fights for us, we also must "fight the good fight of the faith" (Timothy 6:12, RSV). Right off the bat, just out of Egypt, here came a battle for the young nation that had never fought with spears and bows and weapons of war.

God Rewards Obedience

In the face of opposition, first and foremost, Joshua was obedient. In obedience to Moses's command Joshua's strong leadership ability enabled him to mobilize men and to fight the Amalekites while Moses went to the top of a nearby hill to oversee the battle. Exodus 17 is the first detailed mention of Joshua, Moses's minister or "right-hand man." We find that Moses was training and building up Joshua to be his successor even as we are first acquainted with him. After the Amalekites attacked, Moses instructed Joshua to mobilize. Verse 9 says,

> *So Moses said to Joshua, "Choose men for us, and go out, fight against Amalek. Tomorrow I will station myself on the top of the hill with the staff of God in my hand." (Exodus 17:9)*

Our coming together is critical to our success and is the life blood of the church. Moses saw the need to gather the people together, to marshal, to muster, and to mobilize choice men for action. Mobilization takes time, thought, and precision. At this "now" time, a strategy was needed to deal with the threat of annihilation by the

---

[96] George Arthur Buttrick, *The Interpreters Bible, Volume 1.* (Nashville: Abingdon Press), 1991, p. 960.

Amalekites who were intent on driving the fledgling nation into the sea. In the Old and New Testaments, we are reminded time and again about the power of unity and the necessity of our coming together. "Over and over in the Scripture we see what happens when men, even two or three come together in harmony with God."[97]

Joshua obeyed the instruction of Moses. The simple but powerful phrase states: "And Joshua did as Moses told him, and fought against Amalek." There is no mention of weapons, tactics, or numbers. All we are told is that Joshua fought. Simple obedience is a sign of submission, and it is a way of demonstrating that we acknowledge and accept the instruction of a leader. Obedience builds faith, and it is key to victory. Following instruction is fundamental to growth, and as believers, we have this lesson of Joshua following Moses, a leader following a leader.

Wisdom and age dictated that he not climb alone, and it was a good thing he didn't. Moses climbed to the top of what we now know is Mt. Tahuneh. "Even though Mt. Tahuneh, is only 750 feet above the valley floor, it is an arduous climb."[98] Moses was wise enough not to climb the hill by himself and "go it alone" but took trusted assistants with him. "Unfit for the battle themselves, Moses and Aaron and Hur, each of whom was around eighty years of age, retreated from the actual conflict to spend time in intercessory prayer."[99] Aaron and Hur were fellow leaders, confidants of Moses going with him to the top of the hill. Little did Moses know how important the two helpers would be. The help that Aaron and Hur provided was spiritual fellowship and physical support. Aaron and Hur did not talk strategy or engage in small talk. They held up Moses's arms—the first instance of the lifting up of the hands in scripture.

The rod of God represents the standard and the Word of God, and hands raised in surrender to God represent worship. "The rod of God is the sign of sovereign power by which [Moses] was to perform

---

[97] Jamie Buckingham, *A Way through the Wilderness* (Old Tapan, New Jersey: Chosen Books) 1986, p. 110.

[98] Ibid., p. 109.

[99] Herbert Lockyer, *All the Miracles of the Bible* (Grand Rapids: Zondervan Publishing Co.) 1965, p. 69.

all his miracles; once the badge of his shepherd's office, and now that by which he is to feed, rule, and protect his people Israel."[100] This is the same rod that turned into a serpent in the desert. This is the same rod that Moses stretched over the Red Sea. This is the same rod that Moses used to strike the rock to give water to the chiding, murmuring masses. God told Moses, "Be sure to take your rod along so that you can perform the miracles I have shown you" (Exodus 4:17, TLB). It was not just any rod; it was "the rod of God."

Captains Must Get Above The Fray

Moses went up to a high place and positioned himself above the fray in order to intercede and "lift up" Joshua and his men as they fought in the valley. And as Joshua fought in the valley, Moses was fighting on the hill. Moses was interceding for the people, standing in the place between God and man as a mediator. Moses was a figure of Christ, standing in the gap between heaven and earth. Without the intercession of Moses, the battle would have been lost. Without the intercession of our Lord, we would be lost.

Just as our Lord went to Golgotha's hill, Moses went up another hill to confer with God and to entreat the favor of God in the time of trouble. Romans 8:34 says that Jesus died for us and is at the right hand of God, interceding for us. Hebrews 7:25 further states that Jesus is "able to save forever those who draw near to God through Him, since He always lives to make intercession for (us)."

The battle wore long. The text states that Moses lifted up his hands over the battlefield, and when he did, "Israel prevailed."

> *And it came to pass, when Moses held up his hand,*
> *that Israel prevailed:*
> *and when he let down his hand, Amalek prevailed.*
> *But Moses hands grew weary. (Exodus 17:11–12a)*

---

[100] Adam Clarke, *Clarke's Commentary* (New York, Abingdon Press, Volume I, 1973), p. 312.

On the face of it, this seems to be an unexplainable phenomenon, to say the least. What link was there between the raised hands of Moses on the hill and the battling arms of Joshua and Israel's army in the valley? What explanation can be offered? First, the rod of God (v. 9). The rod of God in Moses's hands was the key. Moses was obeying God's command to use the rod as God's representation of His word and power. Second, hands raised signal victory; hands lowered signal defeat. We know that it was a spiritual battle because as long as Moses's hands were raised, Joshua prevailed, but when Moses's hands went down, Amalek prevailed. The battle wasn't about fighting prowess or physical agility; it was a spiritual lesson in obedience. "God made the fortunes of the fight to vary according to the motion of Moses's hands . . . The good generalship of Joshua—first mentioned here—was useless aside from the uplifted arms of Moses, which indicated the recognition of God's part in the conflict."[101]

We don't know how many times it took for the leaders to "figure it out," but figure it out they did. Wise and in-tune, Aaron, Moses's brother, and Hur (supposed by Josephus to be the husband of Miriam)[102] made sure that Moses's arms would stay up until the battle was won.

> *So they took a stone and put it under Moses,*
> *and Aaron and Hur held up his hands,*
> *one on the one side and one on the other.*
> *So his hands were steady until the going down of the*
> *sun. (Exodus 17:12b–13)*

Lift Up Your Hands and Celebrate!

Holding up the hands of a leader is symbolic of assisting, praying for, and being a help to the visionary. This passage teaches that leaders need faithful lieutenants who will come alongside and buttress them physically and spiritually. Implied in our lesson is the need

---

[101] Herbert Lockyer, *All the Miracles of the Bible* (Grand Rapids: Zondervan Publishing House, 1961), p. 69.

[102] George Arthur Buttrick, *The Interpreters Bible, Volume 1* (Nashville: Abingdon Press, 1991), p. 960.

for "followers" to speak well of leaders so that we lift and build them up with our words as well as our actions.

According to Buttrick, the symbol of Moses's hands raised or extended was "not a sign of prayer in our sense of the term. The hand or arm is the sign of power (Genesis 31:29; Micah 2:1); and the outstretched hands of Moses communicate the divine power. . . Whether his arms were stretched upward vertically or outward horizontally, is not clear. Beer *(Exodus, p. 93)* thinks that they were held outward horizontally so that the silhouette of Moses made the sign of the cross. He asserts that the sign of Cain (Genesis 4:15) and the mark placed on the foreheads of those to be saved (Ezekiel 9:4) were also the cross. However it is not Moses's total silhouette but his outstretched arms, communicating the power of Yahweh, that are featured."[103] Nevertheless, he goes on to say that "the idea that certain people by their intercession can protect and inspire others in time of need is a central religious experience. They themselves would say that all they can do is to make themselves channels by which God's power is made available to these other people."[104]

Clarke adds that "we cannot understand this transaction in any *literal* way; for the lifting up or letting down of the hands of Moses could not, humanly speaking, influence the battle. It is likely that he held up the rod of God in his hand as an ensign to the people. We have . . . seen that in prayer the hands were generally lifted up and spread out, and therefore it is likely that by this act prayer and supplication are intended."[105]

While faith without works is dead, works without faith is deadly. If Joshua had fought without Moses's intercession on the hill, the results would have been disastrous. Like Charles Wesley, Moses knew he needed to reach out to God.

> *Father, I stretch my hands to Thee,*
> *No other help I know;*

---

[103] Ibid., p. 961.

[104] Ibid., p. 961.

[105] Adam Clarke. *Clarke's Commentary* (New York, Abingdon Press, Volume I, 1973), p. 390.

If Thou withdraw Thyself from me,
Ah! Whither shall I go? [106]

Raised hands are the universal sign of surrender. Moses's arms raised toward heaven symbolized three things: unconditional surrender, total submission, and complete sacrifice. It means I give up, I will submit to your will and way, and I will sacrifice everything I have. Even though we may be fearful and afraid, this is what we need to do before God: surrender our wills, submit to the will of God, and sacrifice all we have to Him.

"The lifting of hands can be understood to be a symbolic physical action expressing the reaching up of the human heart/mind/being towards God—in the three contexts of worship, prayer or repentance." [107] Further, "since Moses held the staff of God in his hands, he was confessing total dependence on the authority and power of Jehovah. It wasn't Moses who was empowering Joshua and his army; it was the God of Abraham, Isaac, and Jacob, 'the Lord of Hosts.'" [108]

Yet to keep one's hands raised, either to the side, or above the head, is a strenuous exercise. As long as Moses held the rod up in his hands, Israel prevailed, but when he brought his hands down, Amalek prevailed. "We can understand how Joshua and the army would grow weary fighting the battle, but why would Moses get weary holding up the rod of God? To the very day of his death, he didn't lose his natural strength (Deuteronomy 34:7), so the cause wasn't *only* physical.

True intercession is a demanding activity. To focus your attention on God and "pray without ceasing" (1 Thessalonians 5:17) can weary you as much as strenuous work." [109] But it is a necessary work. Lifting up hands was and still is customary for the people of God when they pray. "The effectual fervent prayer of a righteous man availeth much" (James 5:16b, KJV). The Message Bible puts it this

---

[106] *Father I Stretch My Hands to Thee*, Charles Wesley, 1741.

[107] http://www.godswordforyou.com/answers/518

[108] *The Bible Exposition Commentary*: Old Testament © 2001-2004 by Warren W. Wiersbe. All rights reserved.

[109] Ibid.

way: "The prayer of a person living right with God is something powerful to be reckoned with."

Because Moses's hands remained upraised, "Joshua overwhelmed Amalek and his people with the edge of the sword" (v. 13). Dutch Sheets offers this insight: "Another example of prophetic action is Moses holding up the rod of authority at Rephidim . . . Moses was up on the mountain with the rod of authority lifted . . . [The soldiers] probably didn't even see the rod going up and down. It had to do with something going on in the realm of the spirit. The prophetic action was releasing something in the heavenlies. As it did, the authority of God was bouncing back to earth and giving victory to the Israelites."[110] Certainly Moses understood the words of Luther's great hymn, the battle hymn of the Reformation, long before it was written:

> *Did we in our own strength confide, our striving*
> *would be losing,*
> *Were not the right Man on our side, the Man of*
> *God's own choosing.*
> *Dost ask who that may be? Christ Jesus, it is he -*
> *Lord Sabbaoth His name, from age to age the same -*
> *And He must win the battle.*[111]

Likewise, if we try to go it alone and do it alone in our own strength and lean to our own understanding, we will be like Israel at Ai, chased by our enemies in humiliating defeat. And there are times when we know when those near and around us need strength and support.

Paul speaks to the principle of lifting up when he tells the church at Rome and at Corinth about the power of edification. Lifting up implies the need to pick up a brother or sister who is down. Building is a longer term assignment, which requires thoughtful care and planning. Romans 15:2 says, "Let each of us please his neighbor for his good, to edify him" (RSV). Paul was concerned about his approach

---

[110]   Dutch Sheets, *"Intercessory Prayer."* (Ventura, CA: Regal), 1996, p. 220.

[111]   Martin Luther, *"A Mighty Fortress is Our God,"* Verse 2.

in dealing with Corinthian believers, because he says that he wanted to "use the authority which the Lord has given (him) for building up and not for tearing down" (2 Corinthians 13:10, RSV). The same Greek word translated "edify" in Romans 15:2 and "building up" in 2 Corinthians 13:10 is oi)kodomh/n / oikodome (oy-kod-om-ay'),[112] which is an architectural term, and means a building or a concrete structure. It figuratively means confirmation.

In sports, raised hands by a referee during a football game signal a touchdown or a field goal; in a basketball game raised hands represents a three pointer. In every sport, after a goal, a basket, a catch, or a homerun, raised hands are a sign and symbol of celebration. Moses gave us the signal we need to send to heaven that we believe we have victory in hand even though the odds are against us. Moses gave us the recipe for spiritual success and "the how" to defeat a seemingly unbeatable foe.

Exodus 17 was truly a "team" win. Without the effort of everyone, there wouldn't have been victory for anyone. Joshua was obedient and gathered men to fight in the valley. Aaron and Hur stayed up Moses's hands on the hill so that Joshua "discomfited" or overcame the Amalekites. The Living Bible says that Joshua "crushed" the Amalekites. Moses won an astounding upset victory. Israel went from being shot in the back and caught unawares to completely destroying the enemy. The victory was so complete that Moses celebrated the triumph by building an altar and calling it Jehovah-Nissi, the LORD my banner.

Jehovah-Nissi is the first of the compound names of God mentioned in scripture. Banner "has come to mean a flag, or standard, carried at the head of a military band or body, to indicate the line of march, or the rallying point, and it is now applied, in its more extended significance, to royal, national, or ecclesiastical 'banners' also."[113] However, here the word *banner* is "not, in the English sense

---

[112] Biblesoft's New Exhaustive Strong's Numbers and Concordance with Expanded Greek-Hebrew Dictionary. Copyright © 1994, 2003, 2006 Biblesoft, Inc. and International Bible Translators, Inc.

[113] International Standard Bible Encyclopaedia, Electronic Database Copyright © 1996, 2003, 2006 by Biblesoft, Inc.

of the term, an arbitrary token to distinguish one band or regiment of Israel from another, but a common object of regard, a signal of observation, a rallying point to awaken men's hopes and efforts . . . Most importantly, [our] Messiah set forth manifestly as the crucified Savior (Galatians 3:1) is the rallying point for the gathering together in one unto Him of all the redeemed in spirit, in the glorified body also hereafter."[114] Jesus Christ, lifted up on the cross, is our rallying point!

The principle of lifting up is embedded in Christianity. It is the foundation, the bedrock, and the cornerstone of our faith. We do not lift up ourselves, but we lift up Jesus. Jesus said, "As Moses lifted up the serpent in the wilderness, even so must the Son of man be lifted up" (John 3:14, KJV).

> *How to reach the masses,*
> *men of every birth,*
> *For an answer, Jesus gave the key:*
> *"And I, if I be lifted up from the earth,*
> *Will draw all men unto Me.*[115]

Christology is based on the lifting up of Jesus on the cross and to be beaten down; Jesus came to be cursed as He bore our sins on the tree so that we might be reconciled to God. Since He died for us, we are to live for Him. Moses gave us the example of lifted up, outstretched hands. As followers of Christ, we are bound to lift each other up spiritually through prayer, acts of kindness, and obedience to leadership; this cannot be overstated. Put-downs have no place in the life of the believer. Let us never put down; we should only and always lift up, starting with our hands, our heads, and our hearts. Further, Jesus declared, "And I, if I be lifted up from the earth, will draw all men unto me" (John 12:32, KJV).

> *I lift my hands to believe again*
> *You are my refuge, You are my strength*

---

[114] Fausset's Bible Dictionary, Electronic Database Copyright © 1998, 2003, 2006 by Biblesoft, Inc. All rights reserved.

[115] Johnson Oatman, Jr., *"Lift Him Up,"* 1903.

As I pour out my heart
These things, I remember
You are faithful, God, forever [116]

Spiritual Lessons

1. We are to fight the good fight of faith. (Exodus 17:9; Tim 6:12)
2. God knows when we are weak and weary. (Exodus 17:12)
3. We will fully conquer as we depend only upon Him. (Exodus 17:13)
4. God will destroy all of our enemies. (Exodus 17:14)
5. We must give God the credit for all of our victories, great and small. (Exodus 17:15)

---

[116] Chris Tomlin, *"I Lift My Hands."*

CHAPTER 5

Elijah's Fantastic Faith

Then Elijah, the prophet from Tishbe in Gilead, told King Ahab, "As surely as the Lord God of Israel lives—the God whom I worship and serve—there won't be any dew or rain for several years until I say the word!" 1 Kings 17:1, Living Bible

At the customary time for offering the evening sacrifice, Elijah walked up to the altar and prayed, "O Lord God of Abraham, Isaac, and Israel, prove today that you are the God of Israel and that I am your servant; prove that I have done all this at your command. 37 O Lord, answer me! Answer me so these people will know that you are God and that you have brought them back to yourself."

Then, suddenly, fire flashed down from heaven and burned up the young bull, the wood, the stones, the dust, and even evaporated all the water in the ditch!

—1 Kings 18:36–39, Living Bible

Cinderella Man

The riveting film *Cinderella Man* is "the story of James Braddock, a supposedly washed-up boxer who came back to become a champion and an inspiration in the 1930s."[117] "Academy Award winners Russell Crowe and Renee Zellwinger star in this triumphant, powerfully inspiring true story. In a time when America needed a champion, an unlikely hero would arise, proving how hard a man would fight to win a second chance for his family and himself. Suddenly thrust into the national spotlight, boxer Jim Braddock would defy the odds against him and stun the world with one of the greatest comebacks in history. Driven by love for his family, he willed an impossible dream come true."[118]

Elijah Fights For God

Likewise, the prophet Elijah was suddenly thrust onto Israel's national scene and became a champion for God. Elijah was driven by his love for God as his very name means "Yah [short form of Yahweh, the LORD] is God,"[119] or more specifically, "my God is Jehovah (the LORD)."[120] Elijah's name, "meaning 'Jehovah is God,' embodies his whole mission and message. The significance of his name was not only the motto of his life, but expresses the one grand object of his miraculous ministry, namely, to awaken Israel to the conviction that Jehovah alone is God. Old Testament prophets had two important duties to perform:

1. To extirpate [annihilate] the worship of heathen gods in Israel; and

---

[117] http://www.imdb.com/title/tt0352248/

[118] *Cinderella Man*, The film, 2005.

[119] Herbert G. May and Bruce M. Metzger, Eds. *The New Oxford Annotated Bible with the Apocrypha*, (New York: Oxford University Press), p. 444.

[120] W. Phillip Keller, *"Elijah: Prophet of Power"* (Waco: Word Books, 1980), p. 17.

2. To raise the true religion of Jehovah to ethical purity. Elijah gave himself to the first task with great zeal."[121]

He championed right and righteousness, and he overthrew the evils of apathy and apostasy. He became an instant "national" hero for the nation of Israel by winning the showdown on Mt. Carmel—a stunning turnaround victory that became an "instant biblical classic." This larger-than-life prophet is forever a fan favorite of the people of God because "Elijah was a man just like us" (James 5:17, NIV).

In 1 Kings 17, Elijah the Tishbite, without warning, bursts onto the scene. His opening statement in the king's court was simple and direct: "As the Lord God of Israel lives . . ." (17:1a). It was a testimony against the times that there needed to be a reminder that God is still on the throne. God *still* lives! And if God still lives that means that He still reigns, and He still rules. Lest we judge the hearers of Elijah's day, we must acknowledge that, "like ancient Israel in Ahab's day, we are beginning to live and behave as if God does not exist."[122]

Without formal introduction but with a startling conclusion, Elijah proclaimed that the sentence on sin is judgment, and the verdict is that truth will be vindicated. For us and for all time, the blood of Jesus is the truth, and we are vindicated and validated by the Cross of Christ.

Stand For What's Right

The desert prophet stood for right and righteousness and would not, and could not, stand what was wrong. Elijah the firebrand announced the coming of a great famine: "there shall not be dew nor rain these years." To add credence to his credentials, he declared that the famine would only end "at my word" (17:1b, NKJV). "From New Testament references, we learn that the famine lasted three and one half years—long enough to have brought terrible sufferings on the nation" (Luke 4:25; James 5:17).[123] The Message Bible reads, "As surely as God lives, the God of Israel before whom I stand in obe-

---

[121] Herbert Lockyer, *All the Miracles of the Bible* (Grand Rapids: Zondervan Publishing House, 1961), 109.

[122] Ibid., p. 16.

[123] Ibid., p. 108.

dient service, the next years are going to see a total drought—not a drop of dew or rain unless I say otherwise" (1 Kings 17:1).

What a powerful phrase: "unless I say otherwise." Elijah teaches us that God has given us "say" in the affairs of this world. We have the authority to declare and decree, but only at the direction of the Lord. "Thou shalt also decree a thing, and it shall be established unto thee: and the light shall shine upon thy ways" (Job 22:28, KJV).

The sin of apostasy had become entrenched in Israel. "Only a little more than fifty years had elapsed in Israel's history since the new nation had stood at its pinnacle of power under David and Solomon. Less than one short century had seen the kingdom of God's special people retrogress from righteous rulership to the most rampant evil."[124] Proverbs tells us that "when the righteous are in authority, the people rejoice: but when the wicked beareth rule, the people mourn" (Proverbs 29:2, KJV). Thus, "we can only begin to understand the character of God's chosen spokesman of this period, as we see it standing starkly against the darkness of his times."[125]

Dirty Players

"Ahab, son of Omri, the seventh king of Israel, who reigned for twenty-two years, from 876 to 854 (1 Kings 16:28 ff), was one of the strongest and at the same time one of the weakest kings of Israel."[126] "His greatest crime . . . was that he married Jezebel, the daughter of Ethbaal, priest-king of Tyre."[127] Ahab and Jezebel combined to form a dastardly duo previously unseen in Israel. Together, these partners in crime turned the nation from the true God to the worship the false gods of Baal and Ashtoreth. "The Canaanite (or Phoenician) god Baal (16:31–32) was held by his worshipers to be the one who

---

124   W. Phillip Keller, *"Elijah: Prophet of Power"* (Waco: Word Books, 1980), p. 13.

125   Ibid.

126   International Standard Bible Encyclopaedia, Electronic Database Copyright © 1996, 2003, 2006 by Biblesoft, Inc.

127   George Arthur Buttrick. *The Interpreters Bible, Volume 3.* (Nashville: Abingdon Press, 1991), p. 144.

controlled the rain. Elijah intended to show his God, the Lord God of Israel, was the one who really controlled the rain."[128]

Scripture tells us that "Ahab did more to provoke the Lord, the God of Israel, to anger than all the kings of Israel who were before him" (1 Kings 16:34, RSV). "No previous monarch had such a penchant for perverseness as had Ahab. He was literally addicted to evil. Wickedness was a way of life for him. He and his atrocious, fierce queen Jezebel wallowed in lewdness."[129]

As wicked and heinous as this pair was, God raised up a prophet like Elijah who could stand against this evil in bold contrast. The time came for Elijah to speak up and speak out against the rampant evil of his day. The "now" of God descended upon Elijah, and he seized the moment with the boldness of a lion. Heaven countered the fierce evil of Ahab and Jezebel with a more-than-equally-ferocious man of God.

"Fearless, formidable, fierce for the glory of and honor of his God, Elijah did not hesitate to stand alone under the blazing sun challenging his countrymen"[130] and the evil of his times. The sin of Ahab and Jezebel was more than matched by the sanctity of Elijah, for true to scripture, "where sin abounded, grace did much more abound" (Romans 5:20, KJV).

Elijah was different, even strange. He was an outsider who lived outside of the norm, and the norm was apostasy. He lived and operated outside the religious routine. He did not fit in. He was not politically correct and he was not socially acceptable, as he could not accept the status quo. His dress and his habitation spoke of a rugged mountain man. "The people of the rocky hill country were rough, tough, rugged, and perhaps somewhat solemn and stern. They dwelt close to God's creation in crude villages as shepherds rather than in the lavish surrounding of the palace."[131]

---

[128] Herbert G. May and Bruce M. Metzger, Eds. *The New Oxford Annotated Bible with the Apocrypha*, (New York: Oxford University Press), p. 442.

[129] Ibid., p. 13.

[130] W. Phillip Keller, *"Elijah: Prophet of Power"* (Waco: Word Books, 1980), p. 71-72.

[131] J. Hampton Keathley, III, http://bible.org/seriespage/man-elijah-1-kings-17

Several times he is referred to as "Elijah the Tishbite." This is no causal reference and seems to denote his lack of notable pedigree and lineage. We know nothing of his parents or family. "He wore a garment of black camel's hair girded with a leather belt about his waist . . . He stood in striking contrast to the effeminate, perverted Baal priests who wore white linen gowns, high pointed bonnets, and lived on the delicacies of the palace."[132]

Elijah defied the blatant and brazen evils perpetuated by Ahab and Jezebel, that deceitful and desperately wicked duo doomed for destruction. He was not afraid to be singular and separate, to be in the world but not of the world. He was a peculiar prophet, a sanctified seer who did what all believers everywhere are called to do, and that is to

> *Stand up, stand up for Jesus,*
> *ye soldiers of the cross;*
> *Lift high his royal banner, it must not suffer loss.*
> *From victory unto victory his army shall he lead,*
> *Till every foe is vanquished, and Christ is Lord*
> *indeed.*[133]

Miracle After Miracle

Thus the stage was set for a showdown, not only between Elijah and Ahab, but between heaven and earth. It would be an amazing upset of evil, a dramatic comeback to God, and a sweeping turnaround from darkness to light. The turnaround was punctuated by miracle after miracle. Lockyer gives attention to the multiple miracles performed during Elijah's career: "while miracles, declarations of supernatural power, revelations, and prophecies are scattered over almost all the pages of the Bible, we again draw attention to the fact that the majority of miracles are found in groups. As we have already seen, there are those related to Moses and Joshua when the Israelites were becoming a nation; [and] those connected with Elijah

---

[132] Ibid.

[133] George Duffield, Jr., 1818–1888, *Stand Up for Jesus.*

and Elisha as a protest against prevailing idolatry; . . . All of these miracles, particularly prominent in times of historical crisis, reveal a moral and spiritual end, namely, to manifest the sovereignty and power of God."[134]

The multiple turnarounds in Elijah's brief career are notable. Just as a great team makes one great play after another en route to a comeback victory, God performed miracle after miracle in the life of Elijah as the hearts of the people were turned back to God again. First He turned the condition of the land to match the condition of the culture; drought symbolizes the lack of blessing and favor. "If I shut up heaven that there be no rain" (2 Chronicles 7:13, KJV) was a warning to Solomon. Note that it is God himself who said that He could "shut up heaven." Instead of showering down on the idolatrous people, God withheld his rain, which cleanses the atmosphere, provides nourishment for growth, and replenishes the water supply. "The significance of the prophecy of no rain becomes apparent when we understand that those who worshiped Baal believed that Baal controlled the rain. In effect, Elijah cut to the heart of Baalism and challenged their so-called god, proclaiming that the LORD God of Israel controlled the weather."[135]

The natural famine was the result of a spiritual one. Thus, the words of the prophet Amos came to pass even before they were penned: "Behold, the days come, saith the Lord God, that I will send a famine in the land, not a famine of bread, nor a thirst for water, but of hearing the words of the Lord" (Amos 8:11, KJV). "'The shutting up of heaven at the prophet's word was Jehovah's vindication of His sole Godhead,' says Fausset, 'for Baal (though *professedly the god of the sky*) and his prophets did not open heaven and give showers (Jeremiah 14:22). The so-called god of nature shall be shown to have no power over nature: Jehovah is its sole Lord.'"[136]

---

[134] Herbert Lockyer, *All the Miracles of the Bible* (Grand Rapids: Zondervan Publishing House, 1961), p. 109.

[135] Jack W. Hayford, *Spirit Filled Life Bible,* (Nashville: Thomas Nelson Publishers). 1991, p. 513.

[136] Herbert Lockyer, *All the Miracles of the Bible* (Grand Rapids: Zondervan Publishing House, 1961), p. 109.

During the draught God removed his hand-picked servant from harm's way and hid him—first by the brook Cherith and then in the Sidonian city of Zarapheth, the home of Jezebel. Elijah knew full well what David would come to know: "For in the time of trouble he shall hide me in his pavilion: in the secret of his tabernacle shall he hide me; he shall set me up upon a rock" (Psalm 27:5, KJV).

In Zarapheth, God used Elijah to encourage a widow who had lost hope. He miraculously provided an unending supply of oil and meal so that she could feed her son and the prophet. When her son died suddenly, he raised the boy back to life again. God turned the heart of the sin-conscious widow all the way around. After witnessing the power of God she testified: "Now I know that you are a man of God, and that the word of the Lord in your mouth is truth" (1 Kings 17:24, RSV).

The Championship: Good vs. Evil

The climax of Elijah's career was the showdown on Mt. Carmel. Elijah directed King Ahab to call all the people and the prophets of Baal to this summit to decide once and for all who was God.

> And it came to pass after many days, that the word of the Lord came to Elijah in the third year, saying, Go, shew thyself unto Ahab; and I will send rain upon the earth. (1 Kings 18:1, KJV)

Mt. Carmel was the stage for the dramatic closing scene. It was a classic match-up: good vs. evil; right vs. wrong; light vs. darkness. The three and a half years of judgment now complete, it was now time for Elijah to demonstrate before Ahab and all of Israel the power of God. God himself declared that He was in charge: "I will send rain upon the earth." "Elijah, God's sole representative, in his startling costume and dignified mien, who ventured openly to espouse the cause of the God he trusted. On the other side, in the interests of the heathen god, were . . . 450 prophets and 400 prophets of Asherah."[137]

---

[137]   Ibid., p. 111.

Two altars were built, and two sacrifices were prepared and the challenge was given.

> *Then said Elijah unto the people, I, even I only, remain a prophet of the Lord; but Baal's prophets are four hundred and fifty men. Let them therefore give us two bullocks; and let them choose one bullock for themselves, and cut it in pieces, and lay it on wood, and put no fire under: and I will dress the other bullock, and lay it on wood, and put no fire under: And call ye on the name of your gods, and I will call on the name of the Lord: and the God that answereth by fire, let him be God. And all the people answered and said, It is well spoken. (1 Kings 18:22–24, KJV)*

The proof of divinity would be an answer by fire. The prophets of Baal called to their god for six hours, all to no avail. Thus the prophets of Baal failed, as did their god. Jeremiah summed up the foolishness of idolatry in saying that "thy children have forsaken me, and sworn by them that are no gods" (Jeremiah 5:7, KJV). Elijah, on the other hand knew, as did Mahalia Jackson, that God is real:

> *Yes, God is real*
> *He's real in my soul*
> *Yes, God is real*
> *For He has washed*
> *And made me whole*
>
> *His love for me*
> *Is just like pure gold*
> *My God is real*
> *For I can feel*
> *Him in my soul* [138]

---

[138] More lyrics: http://www.lyricsmode.com/lyrics/m/mahalia_jackson

After the high jinks of the false prophets, "with simple, majestic directness, Elijah prays, and fire from heaven falls, burning up the sacrifice and altar and dust and licking up the water in the trench."[139] Elijah prayed

> *Lord God of Abraham, Isaac, and of Israel, let it be known this day that thou art God in Israel, and that I am thy servant, and that I have done all these things at thy word. Hear me, O Lord, hear me, that this people may know that thou art the Lord God, and that thou hast turned their heart back again. (1 Kings 18:36–37, KJV)*

Lockyer may say it best: "Then came Elijah's beautiful, quiet, solemn prayer, so opposite to the wild shrieks of Baal's prophets. The God who answered by fire was to be *the God*, and 'the fire of the Lord fell' and the people fell on their faces and confessed that *Jehovah* was God. The humiliated priests hurried down the side of Carmel but swift and terrible judgment overtook them for all of them were slaughtered."[140]

Whether a lightning bolt or a flash of fire, we are not told. "Some wish to rationalize the fire of the Lord by calling it lightning preceding the rain; but it must be borne in mind that the ancient writer intended to describe a miracle."[141] Buttrick adds that "the fire of the Lord is a supernatural fire, frequently in the OT associated with the appearance of God. Physically speaking, it may have been lightning in this particular case, since the long, hot drought of a semitropical country naturally ends in thunderstorms of a violence not known in more temperate climates. But to give a physical explanation of the

---

139 Merrill C. Tenney, General Editor. *Pictorial Bible Dictionary*, (Nashville: The Southwestern Company), 1976, p. 245.

140 Herbert Lockyer, *All the Miracles of the Bible* (Grand Rapids: Zondervan Publishing House). 1961, pp. 111-112.

141 Herbert G. May and Bruce M. Metzger, Eds. *The New Oxford Annotated Bible with the Apocrypha*, (New York: Oxford University Press), p. 445.

phenomenon does not do away with the miraculous element of it."[142] Thus, the God of Abraham, Isaac, and Jacob, the creator of heaven and earth, gave proof that he was still on the throne. The true and living God once again served notice on all who doubt and oppose Him and his anointed ones.

God upset the status quo and reset Israel's spiritual clock to the correct time. It was time to worship God. Elijah could well have sung this song as an "invitation to discipleship:"

> *Come, now is the time to worship,*
> *Come, now is the time to give your heart.*
> *Come, just as you are to worship,*
> *Come, just as you are before your God, Come* [143]

The people reacted with reverence and fear. "And when all the people saw it (the fire of the Lord), they fell on their faces; and they said, 'The LORD, He is God; the LORD, he is God" (18:39). It was a double declaration. It was a wholesale turnaround.

Rain: The Sign and Seal of Victory

After the destruction of the false prophets, all 850 of them, came the prayer for rain. The prophet boldly declared: "There is a sound of abundance of rain" (1 Kings 18:41, KJV). Elijah sent his servant to look toward the sea, and to report any sign of rain. After six times, the report was, "there is nothing" (v. 42). To hear nothing and see nothing can be demoralizing when something, or just anything, is hoped for. And this is the true test for all men and women of faith.

We know and believe that God is real, that He answers, by fire if need be, and that he will turn the hearts of the people to Him again. The test is to keep believing when "there is nothing;" no sign of rain; no change in circumstance; no fulfillment of the prophecy.

But God did send a sign; after Elijah's servant went to look the seventh time, he saw "a cloud, as small as a man's hand, rising

---

[142] George Arthur Buttrick, *The Interpreters Bible, Volume 3.* (Nashville: Abingdon Press, 1991), p. 158.

[143] Brian Doerksen, *"Come, Now is the Time to Worship,"* 2002.

out of the sea" (I Kings 18:44). "The Bible makes it clear that the rain's withdrawal and then release years later were miracles related to prayer—God's reward for fervent prayers."[144] Lockyer further states that "The God who answered by fire now answers by rain, proving thereby His sovereignty in the realm of nature. The formation and function of rain is ascribed to God's power and direct control (Job 36:27, 28; Amos 4:7; 5:8; Jeremiah 14:22)."[145] And it didn't just rain; it poured. All of a sudden, the sky turned black and the winds wiped fierce. The Bible says that "the heaven was black with clouds and wind, and there was a great rain" (1 Kings 18:45, KJV). James gives us the commentary that

> *the prayer of a righteous man has great power in its effects. Eli'jah was a man of like nature with ourselves and he prayed fervently that it might not rain, and for three years and six months it did not rain on the earth. Then he prayed again and the heaven gave rain, and the earth brought forth its fruit. (James 5:16b–18, RSV)*

Get Back Up and Get Back Going!

The final turnaround was Elijah's recovery from his plunge into despair. Three and one half years earlier, this fierce prophet presented himself at Ahab's court to announce the drought; yet not soon after his triumphant victory over the priests of Baal, Jezebel threatened his life, and he ran for it. "Ahab told Jezebel all that Elijah had done, and withal how he had slain all the prophets with the sword" (1 Kings 19:1, KJV). Note how Ahab told "all that Elijah had done." Apparently there was no true accounting of the events of the day on Mt. Carmel. Ahab evidently slanted the story and did not tell of the wonderful works of God. Keathley poses this query: "I wonder what would have happened if Ahab had seen God in the events on Mt. Carmel and then reported them as such to Jezebel. I wonder what

---

144 Herbert Lockyer, *All the Miracles of the Bible* (Grand Rapids: Zondervan Publishing House, 1961), p. 112.

145 Ibid.

would have happened if he had said, 'I saw God, Yahweh of Israel at work today. I saw him prove to be the true God."[146] God desires truth in the inward part. Ahab falsified the record of the day and perjured himself before God, deliberately inflaming Jezebel. "Unable to hurt the Lord, Jezebel did what Satan and the people always do. She attacked the instrument and gave vent to her hatred and malice."[147]

After a very "high" high Elijah experienced a very "low" low. After using his faith to triumph over the priests of Baal, Elijah's allowed fear to triumph over him. Elijah supernaturally ran seventeen miles from Mt. Carmel to the entrance of Jezreel to herald the victory. In so doing he outran Ahab's chariot. However, when Jezebel reacted negatively and threatened his life, Elijah "went for his life" (19:3). He ran again, but this time his flight was fearful and frightful. "Suddenly, it seems, he is at Beer-sheba, one hundred thirty miles south of Jezreel. [Then], by miraculous divine help, the prophet arrived at Horeb, the place where the LORD revealed the law to Moses."[148]

We remember that Elijah was a man "just like us"; susceptible to ups and downs, highs and lows, ins and outs, and not always the strong, bold man of God he is called to be. "Jezebel's actions were in keeping with her character. It's what we would expect, but not so with Elijah. Elijah's action is totally out of character, but it serves to remind us again of everyone's vulnerability—that we must take heed lest we fall."[149] It is such a comfort to know that "a bruised reed he will not beak." He was strengthened physically and spiritually.

Elijah, like Leah and Naomi and so many other biblical giants, experienced a spiritual low. To counter these times of despair, like Isaiah, all men and women of God are called to obtain "beauty for ashes, the oil of joy for mourning, the garment of praise for the spirit of heaviness" (Isaiah 61:3, KJV). Note that the Word of God calls this

---

[146]   J. Hampton Keathley, III, http://bible.org/seriespage/man-elijah-1-kings-17.

[147]   Ibid.

[148]   Herbert G. May and Bruce M. Metzger, Eds. *The New Oxford Annotated Bible with the Apocrypha*, (New York: Oxford University Press), p. 446.

[149]   J. Hampton Keathley, III, http://bible.org/seriespage/man-elijah-1-kings-194-14.

lowliness a *"spirit"* of heaviness; the NIV renders a "spirit of despair." The New Living Translation tells us that we are to have "festive praise instead of despair." Keathley teaches us that "while there are physical causes, (of depression) and these should be checked out, the most common causes are spiritual."[150]

God turned Elijah's low back to a high. He was down and God's love lifted him back up. No pit is too low, no whale's belly is too deep, no dungeon is too dark that Jesus cannot hear and help. The joy of the Lord is our strength, and He will turn our mourning into dancing again. Elijah was fed by an angel, told to get rest, and then comforted by God on Mt. Horeb. After a great and strong wind, and then fire and then an earthquake shook the mountain, Elijah waited still for direction. But the Lord was not in the wind, or the fire, or the earthquake. After running for his life and wishing for death, "the prophet's spirit was divinely calmed."[151] God did not reprove him or rebuke him. He spoke to him lovingly and gently. He spoke to Him in a "still small voice" (19:12). The margin calls it a "delicate whispering voice."

The sweet voice of the Lord is all we need when down and out. God did not punish him or penalize him. He spoke to him lovingly and gently. Being the comforter He is, he built his prophet back up, and did not tear him deeper down." Likewise, Jesus spoke to Mary when, on Resurrection Sunday, she thought He was still dead and that his body was stolen. Jesus spoke her name only: "Jesus said to her, 'Mary'" (John 20:16). Jesus called to a fearful and confused Cornelius, and is calling to us as well. He told the prophet Isaiah

> *Fear not, for I have redeemed you; I have called you*
> *by name, you are mine.*
> *When you pass through the waters I will be with you;*
> *and through the rivers, they shall not overwhelm you;*
> *when you walk through fire you shall not be burned,*

---

[150]   Ibid.

[151]   Herbert Lockyer, *All the Miracles of the Bible* (Grand Rapids: Zondervan Publishing House, 1961), p. 113.

and the flame shall not consume you. (Isaiah 43:1–2), RSV

John the evangelist told us that "the sheep hear his voice, and he calls his own sheep by name and leads them out" (John 10:3, RSV). When we are sad, we do well to remember that Jesus said our "sorrow will turn into joy" (John 16:20, RSV). One hymn writer told us that

> *There's not an hour that He is not near us,*
> *No, not one! No, not one!*
> *No night so dark but His love can cheer us,*
> *No, not one! No, not one!*[152]

Just as God performed miracles for Elijah, He can and will perform miracles for us, for his grace is just as sufficient now as it was then. At all times, especially when we are at points of extreme, our faith must look up to the Lamb of Calvary, our Savior divine. So we should not sorrow but sing,

> *When I am sad, to Him I go.*
> *No other one can cheer me so*
> *When I sad, He makes me glad,*
> *He's my friend.*[153]

In all instances and in all occurrences of life, we should take courage in the story of Elijah. "Elijah was as human as we are" (James 5:17, NLT) and he gave us a sample of what God can do; he is the example of how to respond to unspeakable and even seemingly insurmountable odds that may be stacked against us. So ask yourself the same question Elijah may have asked himself:

> *Why should I feel discouraged*
> *Why should the shadows come*
> *Why should my heart feel lonely*

---

[152] Johnson Oatman, Jr., *No, Not One!* 1895.
[153] Will L. Thompson, *Jesus Is All the World To Me*, 1847–1909.

And long for heaven and home
When Jesus is my portion
A constant friend is he
His eye is on the sparrow
And I know he watches me.[154]

Spiritual Lessons

1. God will judge all evil. (I Kings 17:1)
2. God will provide for his people as we obediently follow His instructions. (I Kings 17:16)
3. We are to stand for what is right and oppose all that is wrong. (I Kings 18:21)
4. God will answer the prayers of the righteous. (I Kings 18:37-38)
5. We should never be discouraged. If we do become dismayed, we should go to the cleft in the rock and wait to hear the "still small voice" of God. (I Kings 19:12)

---

[154] Civilla D. Martin and composer Charles H. Gabriel, 1905, *His Eye Is on the Sparrow.*

ABOUT THE AUTHOR

 David Hunter is an avid sports fan, a former athlete, and a pastor who successfully connects the dots between God and sports in such a way that encourages and inspires old and young alike. He has taught at numerous churches, conferences, and seminars and is also the author of the inspirational blog, www. GodandSports.net. His teaching and writing focus on the principles of teamwork, discipline, and determination, which are applicable in sports and in life.

David is the Pastor of the Tribe of Judah Miracle Center and holds a BA and MA in Urban Studies from the University of Maryland, College Park, and an M.Div. from Regent University. He served on the Dumfries, Virginia, town council and has traveled to Rome to study the rise of early Christianity and to Uganda to serve on a teaching mission trip.

Pastor Hunter enjoys spending time with his wife, Lisa, taking long walks, watching a sports movie, and serving breakfast meals at a local homeless shelter on a monthly basis. He and his wife have two adult sons, David, Jr. and Daniel Hunter, of whom they are very proud. He is a native of Philadelphia and currently lives in Northern Virginia.

CPSIA information can be obtained
at www.ICGtesting.com
Printed in the USA
BVHW02s0752110918
526661BV00004B/6/P

9 781640 820906